NATURAL HEALING

STRESS

NATURAL HEALING

STRESS

HOW TO SURVIVE IT AND LEAD

A FULLER LIFE · NATURALLY

LEON CHAITOW ND DO

Bramley Books

5001
This edition published in 1997 by Bramley Books
© 1997 CLB International, Godalming, Surrey
All rights reserved
Printed in Hong Kong
ISBN 1-85833-797-6

Project Management: Jo Richardson
Original Design Concept: Roger Hyde
Design: Justina Leitão
Illustration: Laurie Taylor
Index: Caroline Eley
Production: Ruth Arthur, Neil Randles, Paul Randles, Karen Staff
Production Director: Gerald Hughes

CONTENTS

CHAPTER ONE

UNDERSTANDING STRESS

Stress-induced problems now cause more illness and death in industrialized countries than are caused by infectious diseases. We can begin to conteract the harmful effects of stress by learning about how it is capable of contributing to so many different diseases, and how we can change our handling of it.

GOOD STRESS - BAD STRESS

We have learned to believe that 'stress is bad', and it certainly can be extremely harmful to health, but it does not have to be.

Stress can be defined as 'anything which makes a demand on us to respond'. Of course, these demands can be from outside ourselves or self-generated, and we can make excessive demands upon ourselves.

Obvious forms of what is generally under-stood to be stress might relate to work or study, in which demands are urgent, with time deadlines, or where there is great importance attached to the outcome of whatever has to be done.

In an exam or pressured work setting, for example, it is easy to identify with feelings which all too commonly emerge. Perhaps you can recall the feelings such situations have created in yourself – a dry mouth, a pounding heart, a feeling of tension in your muscles (probably in the shoulders, chest and neck areas), excessive sweating, difficulty in taking a deep breath, perhaps an urgent need to use the toilet or even outright panic.

Same stress, different response

These are amongst the likeliest stress reactions when we feel pressured, frightened, anxious or unsure of our ability. Unfortunately, for some people it is how they respond to all life's demands, and so it is no wonder that in time they can become ill as a result. The feelings described, if repeated many times or if present much of the time, can lead to chronic changes in the body that manifest as ill health.

However, the same pressures or demands on someone else might be dealt with in a relaxed, nonchalant way, the task being met with a 'no sweat' attitude and assured competence. For this person, no long-term health risks would result.

The demands of a task might be identical, yet the response can be completely different. Why?

The potential for harmful effects deriving from stress have far more to do with how we feel about and how we deal with the demands we face than they have to do with what those demands are. This is a very important lesson to learn, since it can teach you how to begin to handle those parts of your life that you presently find stressful.

Do we actually need some stress?

Animal studies have shown that colonies of mice made super comfortable, with no need to look for food, become progressively more ill, com-pared with similar colonies in which a certain amount of effort (stress) is required to get food.

The suggestion is that if there are no challenges, demands or stresses in our lives at all, we are as likely to become ill as we would if there were stresses to worry us. This is because a certain degree of stimulus is needed to provide the motivation to function in a way that brings us satisfaction. Some people need a great deal of pressure to provide satisfaction in their lives – they actually thrive on all kinds of situations and conditions that many other people would regard as extremely stressful.

STRESS EFFECTS

CHRONIC EFFECTS, AS A RESULT OF POOR STRESS-COPING

- Hyperventilation; breathing problems; asthma; anxiety; phobias; insomnia

- Poor heat control (feel cold/cannot stand heat); excessive sweating; skin rashes

- Arthritis; chronic muscular pain (neck/shoulders)

- Dizziness; circulatory problems

- Sexual problems (loss of libido/impotency)

- Sleep problems

- Blurred vision and other eye problems

- Ulcers; irritable bowel problems; colitis

- Hypertension

- Allergies; more frequent infections

- Disturbed blood sugar control; diabetes

- Cardiac problems

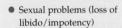

Is stress-coping a learned response?

Why do some people handle stressful situations with ease, and others – the majority – do not? It may have to do with upbringing – early lessons we learned by copying the behaviour patterns and responses of those around us. It may be to do with particular life events that have coloured our sense of self-esteem or confidence. Indeed, it might be to do with a whole series of factors, combining in-born characteristics with the learned responses derived from our life experience to date.

The good news is that we can relearn our responses to stress so that pressures, expectations, demands and problems can be dealt with in ways that offer opportunities rather than threats, a sense of achievement rather than despair and make life a richer experience rather than a battleground.

Once we know that it is not the stress which is harmful but how we handle it, we can begin the job of recreating our previously automatic response, and of learning new, safer, more positive tactics in dealing with stress.

The harm stress can do

The negative effects of stress are so well documented now that it should come as little surprise to learn that a host of ailments, from those that are just a nusiance to serious conditions, including a wide range of emotional and mental illness, are linked to some extent to poor stress-coping (see left).

How we turn what is potentially dangerous into something which is potentially helpful is the quest, since we cannot hope to remove stress in our lives.

The key to surviving the stresses of life lies in the tactics we can decide to employ, which can reduce the stress load, enhance our coping ability and encourage a positive state of health.

HOW STRESS AFFECTS US

We now know that quite different experiences and events produce a stress effect in some people and not in others. One of the best understood aspects of this response is the so-called fight or flight reaction, in which a sequence of responses occurs in the body when we are alarmed by anything – say, a threat or a sudden noise, or any other occurrence that we may think of at the time as alarming.

Whatever the stress factor (known as a stressor) is, information regarding it having been felt, seen or heard is carried by the nervous system to the cortex of the brain where, if it is recognized as a threat or something to be dealt with, signals are sent to another part of the brain – the limbic system. Here, all our emotions are produced – such as fear or anger – and a response is decided on, which might include choosing to run away or preparing to fight or hide, or some other appropriate response.

The General Adaptation Syndrome (GAS) – alarm stage
Once the brain has registered alarm, within a fraction of a second, the sympathetic nervous system is alerted and a barrage of signals are sent which cause adrenalin (a hormone) to be released from nerve endings. This is the alarm stage of what has come to be known as the General Adaptation Syndrome (GAS), and these are just some of the effects that are subsequently produced:

- pupils of the eyes dilate to allow clearer vision

- saliva production and mucous secretions dry up

- muscles tense, the heart quickens and blood pressure rises in preparation for action

- digestive system shuts down to conserve energy

- breathing rate increases to provide oxygen for the muscles

- liver pumps its stored sugar (glycogen) into the bloodstream to fuel all the activity

- blood from the periphery and the internal organs is diverted to the brain and muscles to keep them well supplied during the alarm stage

- adrenal glands (over the kidneys) are stimulated to produce even more adrenalin, to stimulate and maintain increased sympathetic nervous-system activity

This sequence prepares us perfectly to meet danger (stress) – but only if the situation demands fight or flight, as it may have done during our evolution when our ancestors were confronted by threats which required such a simple, direct response. In today's world, such a response could still be appropriate if, by misfortune, we are called on to respond to a criminal attack, for example.

The fight or flight response is not appropriate, however, when we are having to deal with, for example, bad road manners, a stressful work-place situation or a domestic crisis, since in such settings there is often no chance to run or to defend ourselves and so safely release or discharge the potential that has been created by the body to meet the danger. Nowadays, the way we respond to stress may not restore the alarmed muscles, organs and tissues to the state they were in before the stress event. All too often, we bottle up and hold onto the physical tensions and changes that have been created.

GAS – adaptation stage
If stress is repeated and these short-term effects (tense muscles, increased blood pressure, faster

FIGHT OR FLIGHT

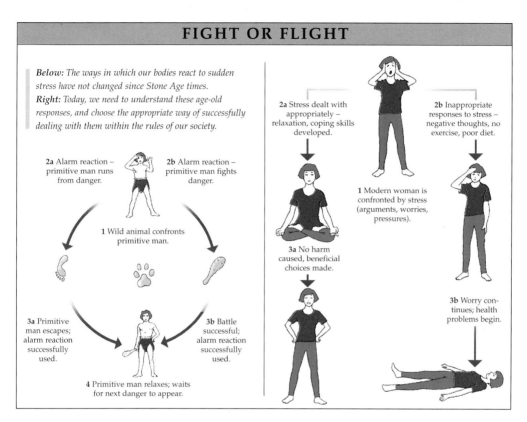

Below: *The ways in which our bodies react to sudden stress have not changed since Stone Age times.*
Right: *Today, we need to understand these age-old responses, and choose the appropriate way of successfully dealing with them within the rules of our society.*

2a Alarm reaction – primitive man runs from danger.

2b Alarm reaction – primitive man fights danger.

1 Wild animal confronts primitive man.

3a Primitive man escapes; alarm reaction successfully used.

3b Battle successful; alarm reaction successfully used.

4 Primitive man relaxes; waits for next danger to appear.

2a Stress dealt with appropriately – relaxation, coping skills developed.

2b Inappropriate responses to stress – negative thoughts, no exercise, poor diet.

1 Modern woman is confronted by stress (arguments, worries, pressures).

3a No harm caused, beneficial choices made.

3b Worry continues; health problems begin.

heart rate, etc.) become continuous, a chronic 'adaptation' situation develops as the body learns to cope with the constant over- or under-activity of particular areas, organs and systems, caused by a host of hormonal and nervous-system changes.

Many symptoms may emerge during this adaptation stage, including impaired vision, disturbance of mucous membranes, tense, tight muscles and joints, heart and blood pressure problems, hyperventilation, elevated blood sugar, digestive and bowel symptoms and depressed immune function.

How long a person can 'adapt to' and cope with long-term stress before becoming seriously ill (the exhaustion stage of GAS) depends on how susceptible or resistant that person is – on their constitution, vitality and previous health status. Eventually, disease is almost certain to occur if the problem is not dealt with. Dealing with it should involve reducing the stress load as well as improving the way the body handles it.

THE RELAXATION RESPONSE

So that we can make sense of how both stress and relaxation responses occur, we need to understand some of the ways in which the nervous system works. It is clear that many of our bodily functions carry on without our awareness – the heart beats, the digestive system digests and a thousand other functions continue automatically day and night, waking and sleeping, while we carry on doing whatever we are doing without us having to think about what is going on inside ourselves.

The autonomic nervous system

These functions are largely under the control of what is known as the autonomic nervous system. This is divided into two parts – the sympathetic and the parasympathetic divisions – which have precisely opposite effects to each other. The impulses from the sympathetic nervous system emerge from the spine below the neck and above the pelvis, while the parasympathetic impulses emerge from the cranial and low back (sacral) areas (see the illustration on the opposite page).

The majority of functions and organs of the body receive appropriate messages from both these divisions, which helps to keep them working in a balanced way. When sympathetic stimulus is received, there is increased activity, while when parasympathetic stimulation is received, there is a slowing down, calming effect – except on digestion and bladder function, which are slowed down by sympathetic activity and speeded up by parasympathetic stimulus. See the panel opposite for the specific effects on the body of the two opposing stimulations

During the fight or flight response to stress (see pages 12-13), when an alarm occurs the sympathetic influence dominates, and the chain-reaction of events which characterize, the fight or flight response takes place.

Just as this stress response produces a predictable chain-reaction of events that can lead to symptoms and ultimately disease if not corrected, so the very opposite – the relaxation response, resulting from the parasympathetic stimulus – produces calming, soothing and health-enhancing benefits.

It is obviously impossible for a muscle to be both relaxed and tense at the same time, and this simple truth helps us to realize that any process or activity which has the effect of relaxing us is going to help to neutralize the negative effects of stress on the body.

Reducing the sympathetic effects

Research into the mechanisms and benefits of massage, relaxation and meditation has shown that when we apply such methods, the para-sympathetic nervous system's influence is increased while the sympathetic nervous system's stimulating effects are reduced. This means that when we relax the body and/or the mind, most of the processes that occur in the alarm and adaptation stage of the General Adaptation Syndrome can be reversed. In this way, the negative effects of prolonged exposure to 'adaptive' stress can be avoided.

Learning to relax

This helps us to understand that one of the key strategies we need to adopt as part of our defence against the inevitable stresses of life is to acquire skills which allow us to relax. Fortunately, there are a wide range of such methods – enough to suit almost all personalities, tastes and lifestyles – and we will be investigating and describing many of these later in the book, particularly in Chapter Four.

STRESS RESPONSE / PARASYMPATHETIC RESPONSE

As you look at this picture of the body and the spine, and the various nerves emerging from it, you should be able to recognize that all the organs and systems of the body are supplied by both parts of the nervous system – the sympathetic portion which responds to stress, and the parasympathetic portion which responds to relaxation. While it is easy to understand that our muscles will tense in response to stress (sympathetic arousal) and relax in response to relaxation (parasympathetic calming), you may be less aware of the many other effects of these two branches of our nervous system, and how they affect every part of our body – as detailed below.

SYMPATHETIC/STRESS EFFECTS

- Iris muscle: Pupil dilated and relaxed

- Heart: Rate and force of contraction increased

- Trachea and bronchi: Lung passages open

- Coronary arteries: Dilated

- Stomach: Peristalsis reduced; sphincters closed

- Intestines: Movements and tone decreased

- Liver: Sugar (for energy) manufacture increased

- Large and small intestine: Mobility reduced; sphincters closed

- Kidney: Urine secretion decreased

- Bladder: Wall relaxed; sphincter closed

- Sex organs and genitalia: Blood vessels constricted

■ areas of sympathetic stress effects

PARASYMPATHETIC/RELAXATION EFFECTS

- Trachea and bronchi: Constricted slightly

- Sex organs and genitalia: Male: erection; female: variable, depending on stage in cycle

- Liver and gall bladder: Blood vessels dilated; secretion of bile increased

- Iris muscle: Pupil contracted

- Stomach: Secretion of gastric juice and mobility increased

- Coronary arteries: Constricted

- Large intestine: Secretions and mobility increased; sphincters relaxed

- Small intestine: Digestion, absorption, juice secretion and mobility increased

- Bladder: Muscle of wall contracted; sphincters relaxed

- Heart: Rate and force of contraction decreased

- Kidney: Urine secretion increased

■ areas of parasympathetic/ relaxation effects

PERSONALITY AND STRESS

Whether particular stress factors harm us or not is decided less by what that stress is and more by how we respond to it. A great many stresses are also self-generated and emerge out of the way we think and behave – from our 'personality types'. The fact is that there are certain human characteristics which can be shown to make stress-related illness more likely. Conversely, there are certain personality features that have a protective influence over the effects of even major stress.

Type A and B personalities
Research – firstly in the USA and later world-wide – has identified so-called type A and type B personalities.

Type A people are quick-moving, impatient, often explosively quick to anger, frequently overworking (probably to deadlines), commonly using excessive levels of social stimulants (cigarettes, alcohol, caffeine, etc.) and are twice as likely as their opposites (type B) to develop heart problems and diseases such as high blood pressure. A type A person tends to believe that they have to constantly prove themselves, whether in work or socially, and their activity reflects this – with work and social schedules that are exhausting and frenetic.

Research shows that behaving in a type A manner is just as risky as smoking or having very high cholesterol levels in the blood. When a type A person also smokes and has a dietary pattern that encourages high cholesterol levels, the risks of developing such diseases is multiplied enormously.

Type B individuals (defined as anyone who is not a type A), on the other hand, are more laid-back and less easily upset, and are far less likely to suffer from such disease patterns. When, rarely, a type B individual does develop heart disease, they are five times less likely than a type A person to have a second heart attack, showing that there are distinct health benefits attached to the mild, calmer, type B behaviour pattern.

Changing your personality type
In later sections of the book (see pages 34-35 and 56-57), we will examine the characteristics of these personality types more closely, and will also see how a type A can 'learn' new habits and turn themselves into a type B.

It has been shown in numerous cases that sometimes a major stimulus to learning these important new habits comes after experiencing a first heart attack. After a coronary (or other serious cardiovascular problem), the need for a change in diet (to quit smoking, reduce salt, animal fats and sugars, etc.) and/or to improve exercise patterns is often obvious, while a need to change other personality-related behaviour patterns may be less clear. However, the fact is that we can learn to change our personalities and may have to in order to survive the stress of life.

What is important at this stage of our under-standing of stress is to recognize that whatever stress factor may be experienced, the ways in which it can affect us are largely decided by what sort of response we offer. Being type A makes it easier for stress to affect us and increas-es the degree of the negative effect. Because type A people are more easily upset and angered, they actually seem to attract stressful situations – just think of 'road rage' as an example.

Hardiness factors
Other personality characteristics which can be protective against stress influences have been identified and are known as 'hardiness factors'. These will also be discussed in greater detail on

pages 34-35 and 56-57, so that new habits and behaviours can be learned in order to protect against the ravages of stress.

The need for change may be more important than you think. There is evidence that not only heart disease is linked to personality and behaviour characteristics (type A), but possibly a wide range of other illnesses.

Self-expression

Personality and behaviour can be major predisposing elements because they govern, or at least influence, potentially harmful conduct, for example in the choice of food habits, drinking, smoking, stumulant use (coffee, tea, chocolate, cola), overwork, inadequate rest and sleep, poor exercise patterns, and so on. There is also the likelihood that particular attitudes and response to people and situations can lead to repression of emotions, such as anger. There is suggestive evidence, for example, that people who 'bottle-up' emotional expression, and who deny negative feelings, have a greater tendency to cancer of various types.

The famous American physician, Bernie Siegel, has described the importance of getting his professional colleagues to learn to express themselves. The typical 'How are you?' met with the meaningless 'Fine thanks', when the person asked is actually feeling lousy, sends all the wrong messages to the immune system. Our immune system is directly under the control of the mind, and studies in this area, known as psychoneuroimmunology, show that it is important to be honest about how we feel, to ourselves and to others.

Siegel asked his hospital colleagues to respond to the 'How are you?' question by giving him, or each other, a grade such as B+ or C-, or whatever was appropriate, followed by a long and meaningful hug. The difference this small change in behaviour made to highly stressed physicians, nurses and ancillary staff was simply amazing, he reports. People began to be honest about how they felt and shared this with those around them. Out of such simple changes come real alterations in our stress levels.

A / B PERSONALITIES

TYPE A – KEY CHARACTERISTICS

- Hyperactive
- Impatient
- Volatile
- Ambitious
- Forceful

Risks:
- As at risk from health problems as any smoker.

- Prone to reliance on excessive use of drugs, cigarettes, alchohol, caffeine, etc., which massively increases the risk of ill health.

- Twice as likely as type Bs to develop heart problems such as heart disease.

TYPE B – KEY CHARACTERISTICS

- Laid-back
- Patient
- Even-tempered
- Non-competitive
- Content

Benefits:
- Many times less-vulnerable than type As to the whole range of stress-induced illnesses (see page 11).

- If type Bs develop heart disease, they are 5 times less likely than type As to have a second heart attack.

LIFE EVENTS AND OTHER STRESSES

We have learned so far in our exploration of stress that it can harm us, while relaxation can help to heal us. How we respond to stress and how our personalities attract or defend against stress are also key elements in the equation. Another factor which can lead to our defences being overwhelmed and illness beginning can be the sheer volume and degree of the stress we are obliged to face, and how long it lasts.

Changes in circumstance

Stress caused by different life events has been examined in great detail over many years, so that we now know that every change in life's circumstances is potentially stressful. Events such as bereavement, divorce, moving home, changing school, getting married, etc. all demand us to adapt – and adaptation is what stress is all about.

If we give a certain number of 'points' to each of these and dozens of other life events, we can calculate our total score over the past six months or year. What has been discovered is that if the score is higher than a certain threshold, our chances of becoming ill increase dramatically. You will be given the chance to calculate your own current stress load on pages 36-37.

Environmental factors

Apart from the obvious stresses of life, and the influence that our personalities and lifestyles have on how we perceive and handle such stressors, there exists a great many less obvious forms of stress which we need to highlight.

These include:

- atmospheric pollution (petrocarbons and heavy metals such as lead in the air we breathe)

- pesticides and other chemicals used in food production

- chemicals used in drinking water purification (such as chlorine)

- multiple toxic chemicals in the home and workplace

- exposure to various forms of radiation

Stress-free choices

Take stock of the conditions and atmosphere of your working and home enviroments, and assess the possible negative effects they could be having on your life. There are many simple, positive steps you can take to avoid or reduce the influence of everyday environmental pollutants and stressors that may, given constant exposure to them, cause significant damage to your health, and will certainly affect your general well-being.

Computer

All electrical machinery produces positive ionization, which can make you feel sluggish. Position negative ionizers in rooms with such equipment to counteract this effect and freshen the air. Use anti-glare screens to ease eye strain. Some screening products may also reduce exposure to extremely low-level radiation emissions from computers. Take regular air breaks, say ten minutes every couple of hours.

Plants

Green house plants, especially large and profusely leaved ones, effectively absorb substances such as benzene and formaldehyde, which are common toxic pollutants found in modern home furnishings. Formaldehyde can derive from wall and roof insulation, synthetic rugs, curtains, wood panelling, fresh paint,wallpaper, cleaning solvents and office copiers, and can cause a variety of health problems.

How well your body handles these stresses and what effects they have on your health status depends, among other things, on how nourishing your diet is, how efficiently your organs of detoxification (liver, skin, bowels, etc.) are functioning, how much exercise you take and your previous medical history.

Anyone who is obliged to travel, work or live in environments and atmospheres that contain chemical fumes, or are poorly ventilated, damp and/or mouldy or excessively hot, cold, or noisy is facing stressors over and above the more obvious stresses of life, and should take appropriate protective, corrective or evasive action.

This is obviously more easily said than done, but the following are just some such possible actions which may offer ways of avoiding toxic exposure.

Avoiding everyday environmental toxins

- Seek out non-toxic home chemicals (detergents, soaps, etc.).

- Filter water from the tap before drinking.

- Choose organic foods as far as possible.

- Introduce ionizers and air-cleansing methods into the home and office.

- Use full-spectrum lighting instead of regular strip or bulb lighting.

- Have plants in the home and workplace to detoxify the atmosphere.

- Avoid prepackaged and processed foods wherever possible.

- Use natural, unchemicalized 'green' products in the home and workplace for carpets, throws, rugs, furniture covering and wallpaper.

- Take antioxidant supplements (vitamins A, C and E mainly) or eat plenty of fresh fruit and vegetables to counteract the negative effects of radiation, many chemicals and heavy metals – see pages 64-65 for more information.

Such precautions are not always available, and may be too expensive or impractical, but they are sometimes options that are open to us but which we neglect through sheer inertia.

Central heating/air conditioning
Heating and ventilation systems are potential sources of fungi, bacteria and other contaminants, and also excessively heat and dry the air. For safety, have all gas, oil and sold-fuel burners/heaters checked to ensure that ventilation of fumes is optimal, and regularly clean all filters. Use humidifiers and foliage plants to help combat excessive dryness, and have windows open at all times. Electric heating is the cleanest and safest.

Curtains and windows
It is now possible to purchase natural (non-toxic) wallpapers and paints, and natural untreated cotton or silk curtains. If any windows cannot be regularly opened for fresh air, have air ducts installed so that an effective exchange of air can take place. Try also to use full spectrum lighting, or spend time outdoors or close to open windows for not less than 30 minutes every day.

Furniture, rugs, floor coverings
Modern furniture can be a ready source of toxic fumes. Try to avoid any plastic or commercially varnished wood. Choose natural materials instead, and apply natural sealants and varnishes wherever possible. Avoid using wall-to-wall synthetic carpeting, and choose instead wool, cotton or other natural-fibre rugs, such as seagrass. Natural linoleum, ceramic or cork tiles are also healthy choices for floor coverings.

CHAPTER TWO

THE EFFECTS OF STRESS

Stress can make you ill or it can simply make your life a living hell. Stress can also be handled without ill effects. What we are looking at in this chapter is evidence of some of the common conditions on which stress has been shown to have a major impact. It will pay you to learn about these possibilities, so that when we look at where you are, personally, in the stress spectrum in the following chapter, you will have a clear understanding of just how important these issues are.

STRESS AND ILLNESS

When we face stress that is short term or prolonged, a series of changes occurs which has enormous implications for our health as our major defence and repair functions (immune system) become seriously compromised. As an example of this, it is well known that during exam periods, students become far more prone to infections. Why should this be?

Energy drain

We have seen on pages 12-13 that a host of instant and often prolonged changes occur during the alarm stage of the stress response (the General Adaptation Syndrome) as the fight or flight response occurs.

Whether this is short term or continuous, the energy required to fuel all these activities is enormous – the increase in muscular tension alone uses vast amounts of energy – and if such changes become chronic, the energy drain will be even greater on reserves and resources. We have seen how the response includes not only increased activity in some areas (muscles, heart, lungs, etc.) but also a shutting down of other activities (e.g. digestion), to conserve energy.

Effects on the immune system

Another way in which the body responds to stress is by economizing on energy used by the many branches of the immune system (see more on this subject on pages 24-25). As a result, immune efficiency declines and infection – amongst other possibilities – becomes more likely. If young, healthy students become ill when faced by stress, what of those who are older and in a less fit state? The elderly for instance, whose immune system would, in part, be acting to keep surveillance on any cell changes that could become cancerous, can become particularly vulnerable when under stress, since the efficiency of the defences becomes compromised.

Stresses such as a bereavement or even prolonged boredom or hopelessness, and indeed anything the person finds stressful, can produce these influences. How can what happens in our own minds affect the physical body in such a devastating way?

A new science has emerged over the past 20 years or so as study of just these mechanisms has been intensively carried out. This is called psychoneuroimmunology (PNI) – the study of the way that psychological factors (our emotions, for example) directly influence our nervous system and our immune system, often by means of changes in our endocrine (hormonal) secretions.

Specific stress-related illnesses

With prolonged stress, tight muscles become chronically fibrosed, short-term digestive changes become chronically entrenched, infections become more likely and slower to heal and a long list of specific conditions (see the panel on the right) are likely to occur – directly as a result of stress not being removed or handled adequately.

When looking at the list (which is not complete because of the contraints of space), remember that the solution to these problems does not lie in medication even if these can help the symptoms, since the causes have to be removed if a real 'cure' is to be achieved.

Dealing with the causes calls for identifying the stress factors and modifying or removing these, as well as improving how we handle stress. In short, the only ways in which true recovery from stress-related illness is to be brought about are to either remove the stress or handle it better.

In the lists that follow, bear in mind that emotional stress is not the only cause, and that it usually combines with other factors (poor dietary pattern, nutritional deficiency, exposure to infectious bacteria or viruses, etc.) to produce the condition, but that stress is commonly a key element in their causation, recurrence or maintenance.

Just how each of these changes emerge in response to stress is not always clear. However, it is important to understand that the fact is that there is no disease process which cannot be made more likely – or more serious – because of stress, and which cannot be helped or removed by a reduction in stress.

STRESS EFFECTS

COMMON STRESS-RELATED PHYSICAL SYMPTOMS AND AILMENTS

- Stomach and bowel problems – dyspepsia, ulcers, constipation, diarrhoea, colitis, etc.
- Migraines; cluster and tension headaches
- Insomnia
- Skin problems – rashes
- Frequent and slow-healing infections
- Muscle and joint pain
- Menstrual and menopausal problems
- Chronic fatigue
- Excessive weight gain or loss
- Loss of sexual interest
- Loss of voice and other speech problems
- Diabetes
- Eye problems
- Breathing difficulties and diseases, e.g. asthma

COMMON STRESS-RELATED PSYCHOLOGICAL SYMPTOMS AND AILMENTS

- Mood swings and irritability
- Extreme tiredness
- Depression and apathy; feelings of hopelessness
- Anxiety – nervous eating disorders
- Loss of concentration
- Explosive temper episodes – tantrums

COMMON STRESS-RELATED BEHAVIOURAL CHANGES

- Dependency on drugs or alcohol
- Problems with relationships
- Problems with work – absenteeism increase, for example

STRESS AND CONSTANT TIREDNESS

During earlier, primitive times, the stresses of life related to finding food and shelter, and learning how to survive in a violent and dangerous world. Come to think of it, nothing much has changed!

In the early days of the human struggle on this planet, a confrontation with a wild animal, a successful fight with it, or flight from it, was about all the choice there was in order to survive. The need for food was another survival essential; if none was found, starvation took care of things.

When confronted with such urgent needs, the ways in which the body responded then were much as they are now – adrenalin was pumped out, muscles tensed in preparation for action, the heart and breathing rate increased to service these muscle needs, while at the same time digestive processes stopped because more urgent needs had to be met. If there was anything in the bowels or bladder, it was rapidly eliminated to reduce any need for these functions to be necessary when extreme action was being called for. Almost instantaneously, many other physiological responses prepared the individual to fight or run away, to preserve life (see pages 12-13).

The modern equivalent is, of course, the struggle for survival in a concrete jungle, and although the physiological responses remain the same – our muscles tense, while blood pressure, heart and breathing rate are rapidly increased, and so on – the actual response we make to danger usually, for practical and legal reasons, cannot be the same as in primitive times. We cannot take a club to the traffic warden, the boss or the spouse. Nor can we usually physically run away from confrontations.

Muscle tension and fatigue

So there is often no resolution to the build-up of this 'preparation for action'. Instead, we tense our muscles and hold them tense. We prepare for action but do not act. If this series of physiological responses is repeated many times a day, until the muscles become permanently tense, the blood pressure permanently high, the respiration permanently shallow and high in the chest, the wastage of energy becomes profound and constant fatigue is felt.

Muscles are the largest energy-users in the body, and if some (often many) of these are kept in a state of constant tension ready for action, the wastage of energy is profound.

Sleep disturbance and fatigue

When we are under stress and are coping poorly with it, other fatigue-inducing events may occur. One of the commonest is disturbed sleep. Feeling tired all of the time – a common sequel of being 'stressed' – and yet not being able to sleep properly is all too common. And it is not just tiredness that results.

During deep sleep (a period of sleep when alpha brain waves are evident), the pituitary gland which lies deep inside the head secretes a hormone known as the Hypophyseal Growth Hormone (HGH for short). Among the very important jobs this hormone has to perform is to see that tissue repair is carried out efficiently, something that happens mainly during our sleep. If HGH is not being adequately produced, we will feel more tired, our tissue repair (mainly muscle) will be inadequate and a number of ailments may appear, including the onset of chronic muscle pain (fibromyalgia).

Under-oxygenation and fatigue

When we feel anxious, it is common for our breathing to become very shallow and for the

HOW STRESS CAUSES TIREDNESS

- Inadequate supply of oxygen to the brain due to shallow breathing causes lack of concentration.

- Brain recognizes need for action, but body held continually in a no-action alert state.

- Blood pressure and heart rate permanently increased.

- Breathing permanently shallow and high in chest, causing lethargy.

- Lack of deep sleep prevents inadequate production of Hypophyseal Growth Hormone (HGH), causing fatigue.

- Inadequate supply of Hypophyseal Growth Hormone (HGH) fails to fully repair muscle tissue, leading to chronic pain.

- Muscles permanently tensed (causing wastage of energy) and consequently require additional oxygen, but are receiving less than they normally need due to shallow breathing. Aches and fatigue result.

Steps to recovery

1 Relax muscles through deep-tissue techniques, as used by osteopaths, chiropractors, massage and physical therapists (see pages 72-73).

2 Stretch and normalize tissues that have become shortened in yoga exercises (see page 73) and self-stretch exercises (see pages 48-49).

3 Re-educate your breathing patterns (see pages 42-45 for exercises), to ease fatigue and profoundly relax the whole system.

4 Take up aerobic exercise (see pages 62-63 for guidance) to enhance general health and reduce stress levels.

Left: Learning to breathe in ways that are both relaxing and energizing can be helped by simple stretching. As you breathe in, the arms are opened wide to allow expansion of the chest. They are brought together again as you breathe out, to encourage full exhalation.

tissues of the body in general, and the brain in particular, to receive inadequate oxygen supplies. The combination of muscles which are tense and which therefore require more oxygen actually receiving less oxygen than they need because of a disturbed breathing pattern makes them feel achy and far more easily fatigued than normal.

Overall, anyone who breathes shallowly is likely to have a sense of lethargy, and will probably find it difficult to concentrate because of brain oxygen deficit. The whole problem becomes something of a vicious circle because the muscles that will become most affected when upper chest breathing is a habit are those of the chest, neck and shoulders (they are being overused). As they become more and more tense and fibrotic (and probably painful), so their ability to work efficiently is greatly reduced at the very time that greater demands are being made. Fatigue, pain and under-oxygenation are all to be expected when this happens.

STRESS AND THE IMMUNE SYSTEM

Doctors in Florida, in the United States, studied people with a tendency to herpes outbreaks, to find out whether it was possible to predict when these would occur. What they discovered was that if they kept track of and measured a person's 'life event' stress scores (see pages 18-19 and 36-37), they could predict fairly accurately when an outbreak of herpes was likely – and the higher the score (which means the more stress), the more probable the outbreak was.

Vulnerability to infection

We also know that at exam time, students become more vulnerable to infection – a clear sign that their defences are weakened. To prove just what is happening in this situation, research has been carried out in which blood samples were taken from medical students six weeks before and during the days of their exams, several times a year. Whenever the blood samples were taken, the students also completed a simple checklist which summarized behaviour patterns (how much sleep they were getting, dietary changes, etc.), as well as any symptoms they might be having (digestive problems, distured sleep patterns, etc.). The results were dramatic. They showed that at exam time, compared with their normal student life away from exams and whether or not they had increased their coffee intake, whether their eating patterns had changed or not or whether they were depriving themselves of sleep to cram or not, their immune defences against bacterial and viral infection (Natural Killer cells, for example) were all significantly depressed, which made them far more vulnerable to infection.

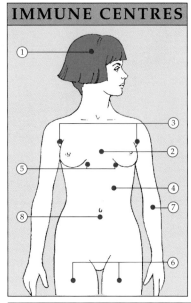

IMMUNE CENTRES

1 *Brain*, which influences all other immune-system centres.

2 *Thymus gland,* which manufactures 'T'-cells that defend against infection.

3 *Lymph nodes*, where many immune system cells are manufactured and stored.

4 *Spleen* – a large lymph gland – where specific immune-system cells are formed and stored.

5 *Lungs*, which form part of the body's defence (immune) system.

6 *Bone marrow and blood vessels*, where 'B'-immune cells are made.

7 *Skin*, which acts as part of the defence potential of the body.

8 *Gastrointenstinal tract*, where many immune functions are carried out.

Consequences of emotional stress

These tests show that emotional stress makes us less able to defend and repair ourselves against infection and degenerative conditions such as arthritis, heart disease and cancer. There is only so much energy to go around, and when we are in the alarm or adaptation phase of the stress reaction (GAS – see pages 20-21), it is our defence and repair capabilities that suffer.

STRESS AND THE DIGESTIVE SYSTEM

One of the most common of all areas of the body where stress has serious and often prolonged harmful effects is the digestive system. We have seen how during the alarm stage of the stress

1 *Oral cavity* (mouth, palate, salivary glands, phraynx), where food processing begins by being broken down and mixed with saliva.

2 *Oesophagus*, the tube leading to the stomach.

3 *Liver,* which produces bile to help digestion (fats in particular), and which stores and processes nutrients, and detoxifies.

4 *Pancreas*, which produces digestive enzymes.

5 *Stomach,* where the action of food processing begins.

6 *Small intestines,* where digestion continues.

7 *Large intestine,* where remaining water is absorbed and excreted material is stored.

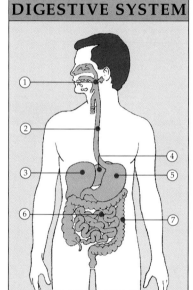

DIGESTIVE SYSTEM

Irritable Bowel Syndrome (IBS)

The characteristics of IBS include indigestion, bloating, wind, nausea, abdominal pain, constipation and/or diarrhoea – with or without pain. About half of such patients, who are far more likely to be female than male, after being examined by medical specialists are found to have no obvious disease.

Why does this condition develop? Research shows that IBS patients are more likely to also be depressed and anxious – clear signs of stress influence – although it may be that these symptoms (anxiety, etc.) are the result of the bowel problem rather than the cause. These patients are commonly high scorers on the 'life events' scale (see pages 18-19 and 36-37), while almost half report that they suffered a loss or threat of a loss (bereavement, job, etc.) shortly before the onset of their symptoms.

Treatment

Medical treatment of IBS usually involves use of drugs to control intestinal function, plus dietary and lifestyle (alcohol consumption, smoking, etc.) advice. Research has shown that when stress-coping psychotherapy sessions that focus on the safe handling of interpersonal conflicts, better stress management etc. are added to the standard medical approach, results are far better. In a wide range of digestive problems, ranging from gastric ulcers to IBS, there is evidence that stress can cause or maintain such conditions, while stress reduction can help to heal them.

response, there is a shutting down of digestive secretions and a diversion of blood supply from the digestive system as a whole towards the muscles, heart, brain, etc. (see pages 20-21). In chronic stress conditions, these changes can produce serious symptoms in some individuals – including what is called Irritable Bowel Syndrome (IBS), also known as 'spastic colon', 'irritable colon' or sometimes 'mucus colitis'.

STRESS, HIGH BLOOD PRESSURE AND CHOLESTEROL

When stress is excessively present in our lives, the responses of the body involve increased blood pressure together with more heart and lung activity, to prepare for and to meet any possible threat. In such a response, an increased production of adrenalin occurs, the hormone which is the trigger for the alarm stage of the 'stress response' (see pages 12-13). Adrenalin increases the amount of blood being pumped by the heart with each beat, and so, as a safety measure, the tension in the walls of the blood vessels is increased to protect them. These changes increase blood pressure, which measures both the pressure of blood as it is pumped from the heart – systolic pressure – as well as the pressure in the blood vessels them-selves between heart beats – diastolic pressure. Another stress effect is the conservation by the kidneys of sodium (salt) and water, which further increases blood pressure.

The effects of high blood pressure

High blood pressure levels can lead to minute areas of damage to the blood vessel walls. One of the ways in which the body responds is to mobilize stored fats which are used to both provide additional energy as well as to form small plaques of cholesterol that are employed to repair the damage. High blood pressure is then made worse, since the repaired areas will usually be slightly narrower, causing even higher pressure.

As the stress responses become more and more chronic, great strain is placed on the heart, the blood vessels and the body as a whole, and heart attacks or strokes become more likely. Cholesterol is needed in every cell of the body, but we do not need it in excessive amounts, and a high stress level (as well as a host of possible dietary indiscretions) increases cholesterol levels.

Combatting the effects

In order to reverse the potential dangers of high blood pressure, stress factors need to be removed wherever possible, and habits that encourage further damage should be altered. If, for example, as a response to feelings of being under pressure, having tight deadlines, being unhappy in domestic or job settings, of holding unexpressed angers, fears or anxieties, someone becomes dependent for diversion or comfort on alcohol, excessive amounts of food or cigarettes, they are compounding the stress and making a breakdown of the system more likely. The safest and most effective answer is to apply stress-reducing strategies, to learn relaxation and/or meditation methods, to improve dietary, sleep and exercise habits and to eliminate bad habits (smoking, alcohol or caffeine dependency) so that the external stresses are defended against, rather than being added to.

STRESS AND HEADACHES

One of the most widespread ailments affecting humans is headache, and among these, migraine and contraction headaches are the commonest. Contraction headaches occur when muscles in the neck, or attaching to the head, are held in a tense state. These tense muscles impede normal circulation to and from the head and irritate local nerves, as well as often developing localized areas of extreme sensitivity, called trigger points. Depending upon where these are sited, they can refer pain into the head, face or eyes, which can last for hours or days on end.

Trigger points

Research shows that trigger points are a part of the cause of all chronic pain. Any form of stress affecting the person – physical, emotional, toxic, climatic, etc. – will make the trigger, and therefore the referred pain, more active. The stress does not have to be directly linked to the area housing the trigger to do this. Massage, stretching and soft tissue manipulation can ease trigger points, but if the stress patterns that produce them continue, the pain will return.

Below: The site of a commonly occurring trigger point in the shoulder (trapezius) muscle that can cause headaches and pain in the face.

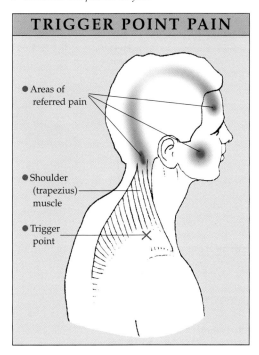

TRIGGER POINT PAIN

- Areas of referred pain
- Shoulder (trapezius) muscle
- Trigger point

Migraine

Classic migraine headaches, on the other hand (there are various types), are usually one-sided and may be preceded or accompanied by flashing lights, zigzag lines or blurred vision as well as nausea and sensitivity to light, and can last for hours or several days.

The link between stress and all sorts of headache is clearly established. However, in many instances the headache only arrives as the stress is ending rather than when, or soon after, it occurs.

Biofeedback

The proof that stress is linked to the causation of such headaches has been shown in many clinics where relaxation methods are taught, and where people can often learn to 'switch off' their pain. In particular, a method of relaxation called biofeedback has been used. This uses a small device which gives the person attached to it information regarding one of their functions, such as the temperature of the skin on their hand, or the amount of electrical resistance in the skin on their forehead.

Migraine sufferers are taught to 'warm up' one of their hands by means of mentally induced activity, which they can observe on the 'feed-back' machine (hence the name 'biofeedback'). Contraction headache sufferers learn to change the electrical resistance of the skin in specific muscles on their forehead in the same way.

Progressive muscular relaxation

Other methods that have been shown to help headaches to be controlled or eliminated include progressive muscular relaxation (see pages 46-47). However, it must be noted that migraines related to menstruation, as well as cluster headaches, do not seem to respond very well to these methods.

STRESSFUL BREATHING AND ANXIETY

When we breathe fully, we not only take in oxygen but we also eliminate carbon dioxide. Exhaling carbon dioxide is far more important than you might think, since it is not just 'used air' but a vitally important compound which takes part in maintaining the delicate stability of the body's internal environment in ways that impact directly on our health and feelings.

Normal breathing mechanisms

When we exert ourselves, the muscular and general increase in activity creates wastes, such as lactic acid, which increase the levels of acidity in the bloodstream. When it is in a normal healthy state, the bloodstream should be just barely acidic, and any strong build-up of acidity can prove dangerous. The elimination of excess levels of acid is, therefore, one of the priorities of our self-maintenance systems, and this is achieved to a large extent when we breathe heavily, puffing and panting, during exertion. In doing so, we breathe out vast amounts of carbon dioxide, which derives from carbonic acid in the bloodstream. In this way, acid is brought down to a safe level.

The effects of stressful breathing

When, however, we breathe in an 'upper chest' manner while we are not exerting ourselves – something which is extremely common in stressed individuals – we tend to remove too much acid and so create an alkaline bloodstream, as inappropriate amounts of carbonic acid turn into carbon dioxide to be breathed out.

As the bloodstream becomes slightly alkaline, a chain reaction occurs in which we will immediately feel apprehensive and anxious – something which tends to reinforce the unbalanced breathing pattern even more. At the same time, other symptoms will occur – the reduced (because breathing is shallow) levels of oxygen in the blood will be more tightly bound to the blood cells that are carrying them, and the blood vessels in the head will narrow, restricting blood flow. The end result of this is a greater sense of anxiety, a 'foggy brain' (lack of concentration and memory lapses) as well as a profound sense of fatigue (see pages 22-23).

A further increase in symptoms often occurs in which the stress-induced breathing imbalance leads to further anxiety, which commonly leads to panic attacks and even, in time, to phobic behaviour.

The hi-low test
To test for upper chest breathing pattern, sit with one hand on your upper chest and the other hand on your stomach. On breathing, the lower hand should move forwards. This is an indication of the correct diaphragmatic pattern. If the upper hand moves first or the most – especially if it moves towards the chin — this indicates poor breathing function and a need to practise the self-help methods presented on pages 42-55.

Self-help treatment

Improvement can best be achieved using several different approaches. Relaxation exercies are helpful, but these are seldom fully successful unless bad breathing habits have also been improved. Relaxation, meditation and especially breathing retraining (pages 47-48) are the best ways forward when such conditions exist.

Sleep is one of the first of our functions to suffer when we are stressed. An inability to get to sleep, a periodic waking up through the night or a normal length of sleep but a shallow and fitful pattern of rest are all extremely common. Sleep is a vital restoration period for the body and the mind, and any long-term disturbance produces a further list of negative effects, and adds to the discomfort and unhappiness of periods of stress.

The functions of sleep

Among the many functions that take place during sleep is the release from the pituitary gland of specific 'growth' hormones. These act to encourage growth during that period of our lives when we are developing. However, in adult life their action is to control many of the repair functions that go on during our sleep. If the hypophyseal growth hormone (HGH) is deficiently produced, there is likely to be a gradual development of muscular aches and pains as well as a general feeling of being unwell. Many people with chronic fatigue syndrome or the widespread muscular pain of fibromyalgia are ill largely because they have lost their sleep pattern and with it the normal production of HGH.

Restorative measures

Restoring more normal sleep patterns when we are stressed is therefore of major importance, and a wide range of approaches exist which can help to achieve this, ranging from the methods previously touched on – especially breathing retraining, relaxation, meditation and visualization. Herbal products can safely ease feelings of undue tension (valerian, passiflora, chamomile), as can a number of nutrients (calcium, magnesium, vitamin B-complex).

SLEEP-ENHANCING MEASURES

- regular exercise – both aerobic and gentler stretching methods such as yoga or t'ai chi

- structured work, rest and play patterns

- sound (quality, quantity and timing of) eating habits – try never to skip meals

- avoidance of stimulants (caffeine, for example)

- dealing with emotional issues through counselling or therapy

- cultivation of relaxing, creative hobbies (music, gardening, painting, etc.)

- (re)introduction of sleep time rituals (bath, music, late-night snack, etc.)

- regular massage or aromatherapy sessions

- after-lunch rest (or sleep) – even if it is for only 15 minutes

Medication

If stress is not going to be allowed to actually make you ill, it is important to ensure that your sleep pattern is restored. Should this include the use of sleeping tablets? Only if absolutely necessary, and then for a short period only (after a recent shock, for example, for a week or so) and only under expert medical guidance.

While it is usually safe to take extra calcium and magnesium and/or a vitamin B-complex purchased from a health store or pharmacy, you might need special advice or other supplements. Consult a qualified nutrition counsellor or a naturopath or other suitable professional.

YOUR BODY SIGNALS

On pages 20-21, we have seen how symptoms can appear as a result of stress overload. To see how your own body and mind is standing up to your present stress load, make a list of any symptoms you might have – however unimportant you may consider them. List anything which is out of the ordinary, whether serious enough for you to have sought medical advice or not.

Is stress affecting your health?
You may have noticed, for example, that you have been waking with less energy and verve than you used to, that your appetite for food is not what it was, or interest in sex is declining, that you get periodic indigestion, odd aches and pains, have dandruff, and so on. List these signs or symptoms, and next to each try to think of reasons in your lifestyle and behaviour that might be contributing to them.

- Energy decline/loss of appetite for food and sex: Which stresses in your life might be contributing to these changes?

- Indigestion: Are you eating too quickly? Are you eating too much junk food? Are you not chewing well enough? Is worry the cause?

- Frequent colds: Are you not getting enough sleep or exercise? Is anxiety over your job a factor?

- Aches and pains: Are repressed anger and/or frustration possible causes?

The ideas you come up with as to connections between your symptoms and the stresses in your life may not always be accurate, but it would be a useful exercise to try to see whether, after what you have read so far in this book, you are able to make any associations at all.

Evaluating symptoms
The fact is that there are seldom direct links between any single stress and a specific symptom. More usually, a combination of stress factors interact with your unique characteristics to produce whatever symptoms your particular susceptibilities dictate.

Remember also that all symptoms are not necessarily 'bad' – they may actually represent evidence of your body dealing with problems. For example, the symptoms we get when we have an infection and the immune system is fighting microorganisms may not be fun, but without the temperature and all that flows from it we might not survive!

Listening to your body's messages
Symptoms are usually signals or messages, and we should listen to them since they may represent early warning of worse to come unless we do something about the causes, which are all too often well within our control (see pages 38-39).

Ask yourself whether you 'hear' and respond to the signals your body sends you many times each day.

- When you are thirsty, do you always get something to drink?

- When you are hungry, do you always eat or do you skip meals at times?

- When your bowels indicate a need to empty, do you sometimes/often ignore this signal?

- Do you pride yourself on 'bladder control', and ignore urges to urinate?

- Do you ignore tiredness – staying up later than sleep needs demand, or using stimulants (coffee, for example) to 'keep you going'?

- If you feel a yawn coming on, do you attempt to suppress this?

- Is your work load so intense that when you have a break you don't know how to stop?

Rhythms of life cannot be denied without penalty. Yes, you can survive by doing all of the ignoring listed above, but the price you will pay will be a gradual decline in efficiency brought on by these stressful demands, as your normal functions slowly adapt to a less efficient pattern of living, and sooner rather than later illness will develop.

Common body/mind stress responses
The various interpretations given below as to how the body/mind may respond to different emotional states represent possibilities and are certainly not the only possible reasons for problems of this sort. Ask yourself whether any of these suggestions could be accurate in your own case, or if not, what you consider might be background reasons contributing to whatever symptoms and signs you are currently experiencing.

Remember that when we look at the actual way the body handles strong emotions, both positive and negative, such as fear, anger and joy, they are remarkably similar.

- Headaches may result from feelings of tension and extreme frustration.

- Pain in the face, mouth or jaw may represent unexpressed anger.

- Throat problems can also be linked to powerful feelings that are unspoken.

- Shoulder symptoms may represent overload. Have you taken on too much?

- Stomach and digestive problems can relate to almost any apprehension (apart from when they are due to poor eating habits), relating to 'something' that is going to happen or that is feared; or the cause may lie in unresolved or unaccepted conflicts.

- Low back problems may relate to exhaustion, perhaps due to not enough rest or exercise plus excessive work, or to strong fear or guilt feelings.

- Leg problems may be linked to fear of change, or to inflexible attitudes.

- Arm problems might connect with feelings of anger and frustration.

What we need to do is to learn to listen to our body, to hear its complaints and to make appropriate adjustments to our life and the way we live in order to meet more effectively the needs we have for adequate diet, rest, exercise and peace of mind. Answer the questionnaire at the beginning of the next chapter to gauge how you, personally, handle stress.

Keeping a sense of proportion
While we have seen here just how vital it is to listen to our bodies, it is also important not to become obsessed about every sign and signal. So how can you establish a balance between listening to your body's signals and ignoring them? Apply common sense and remember that odd twinges are probably meaningless. It is only when any problem persists that you should investigate its causes. Usually, the best way of doing this is to look at the bigger picture – yourself in the context of your work, your relationships and your commitments.

CHAPTER THREE

YOU AND STRESS

We have already seen (pages 20-21) how stress can produce a range of effects, both physical and emotional. In this chapter, we will be evaluating some of the influences of life events, personality, lifestyle and environment on your particular stress load. To learn more about yourself, answer the questionnaires presented in this chapter honestly. Remember that there are no 'wrong' or 'right' answers – only accurate ones which might help you to understand how stress is present in your life, how you deal with it and how it may be affecting you right now.

ANALYSING YOUR STRESS LOAD

Once you have completed the following questionnaire, and having referred back to pages 20-21 to see if any of the conditions itemized are present in your list of health problems, continue with this chapter and then move onto the many solutions on offer in Chapter Four.

If you apply some of these safe and helpful suggestions, come back to these questionnaires in six months' time and re-evaluate the questions and your answers – and surprise yourself at how much you have changed for the better!

1 Ask yourself whether you feel more stressed now, today, than six months ago:

at home	at work	socially
YES/NO	*YES/NO*	*YES/NO*

2 Refer to the text on pages 20-21 in particular, as well as to all the other information contained in Chapters One and Two, and list here the physical and mental/emotional conditions from which you suffer and which you believe might be stress-related. Most importantly, give a score to the symptoms out of 10, where 0 = no symptom at all,

5 = moderately severe symptoms and 10 = very severe symptoms.

Physical symptoms

.... *(score   )*
.... *(score   )*
.... *(score   )*
.... *(score   )*
.... *(score   )*
.... *(score   )*
.... *(score   )*

Emotional symptoms

.... *(score   )*
.... *(score   )*
.... *(score   )*
.... *(score   )*
.... *(score   )*
.... *(score   )*

3 Have you developed any stress-related behavioural changes such as:

excessive drinking/drug use?	*YES/NO*
increased signs of temper?	*YES/NO*
problems at work or domestically?	*YES/NO*

4 Do you believe that stress affects you:

Very little?	Moderately?	A great deal?
YES/NO	*YES/NO*	*YES/NO*

5 What do you think are the major causes of stress for you:

Work situations?	YES/NO
Relationship situations?	YES/NO
Economic factors?	YES/NO
Social problems?	YES/NO
Health problems?	YES/NO
Other? (specify)	

6 Based on what you have read so far in this book, and learned elsewhere, how do you rate your stress-coping skills?

Weak?	YES/NO
Average?	YES/NO
Good/above average?	YES/NO

7 List current stress-coping strategies which you use regularly:

Drinking tea, coffee, alcohol, and smoking?
YES/NO
Taking prescription medication (tranquillizers, etc.)? YES/NO
Talking through your problems with someone you trust? YES/NO
Making sure that you have regular recreational breaks? YES/NO
Avoiding mixing home and work life (no work taken home)? YES/NO
Taking regular exercise (walking, swimming, sport, etc.)? YES/NO
Having a creative hobby (painting, gardening, sewing, writing, etc.)? YES/NO
Practising yoga techniques, t'ai chi, aikido or other similar system? YES/NO
Regularly doing breathing, relaxation or meditation exercises? YES/NO

8 How many days were you sick in the past year where you believe your illness was stress-related?

9 The events that occur in our lives, good and bad, require that we adapt and change, and are therefore by definition 'stressful' – even if we are enjoying them. The way we respond to what happens to us is, as we have seen, more important than the stress event itself. Rather than checking a list of possible 'events' which may or may not have been stressful had they taken place in your life, answer the following key questions honestly to see whether you handle stress positively or negatively. Imagine that:

You are experiencing sexual difficulties (loss of interest perhaps). Do you:

a worry and fret	YES/NO
b speak frankly to your partner	YES/NO
c seek professional advice	YES/NO

You are told that you will become redundant in one year's time. Do you:

a worry and fret	YES/NO
b start looking for a new job immediately	YES/NO
c start to retrain to do something different that you have always wanted to do	YES/NO

You develop a vague numbness in your left arm at times. Do you:

a worry and fret	YES/NO
b read up on the possible causes and treat yourself	YES/NO
c seek professional help	YES/NO

If any of your answers were a, you might like to think about how sensible or silly these decisions would be compared with the alternatives – b and/or usually c always being the best options.

Once you have honestly answered all the questions on these two pages, you will have a better idea of aspects of your current relationship with stress. As you follow the remainder of this chapter, you will gain an even better understanding of aspects of your life and behaviour that you might usefully wish to modify.

ANALYSING YOUR PERSONALITY TYPE

By definition, if you are not a type A person then you are a type B.

Why does this matter? Because being type A – or rather behaving in a type A way – is a major stress load all on its own (see pages 16-17).

However, you can change from type A to type B if you want to – partly by copying the habits of type Bs and by dropping or modifying type A characteristics, as well as employing anti-arousal, calming, stress-reducing methods such as those detailed later in Chapter Four, including relaxation, meditation and breathing exercises and lifestyle modification (diet and other habits – see pages 64-65). Sadly, deciding to make these radical changes may not happen until a real scare occurs – a heart attack, for example – when damage will already be partly irreversible. The time to change is before trouble strikes, and completing the questionnaire on pages 32-33 could alert you to the need for change. Test whether you are indeed type A by answering the following questions too.

ARE YOU A TYPE A PERSON?

Are you irritated by delay, say at a store checkout or in traffic?   *YES/NO*

Are you impatient – interrupting people before they finish speaking?   *YES/NO*

Do you walk, talk, eat and/or move quickly?   *YES/NO*

Do you set and like to work to deadlines? *YES/NO*

If you are not active, do you get restless and edgy?   *YES/NO*

Do you often find yourself doing more than one thing at a time?   *YES/NO*

Do people anger you easily?   *YES/NO*

Are you forceful or generally dominant in your behaviour?   *YES/NO*

Are you extremely competitive – do you have to win or succeed?   *YES/NO*

Do you crave recognition from your colleagues at work?   *YES/NO*

Do you set yourself strict deadlines?   *YES/NO*

Are you particularly time-conscious, and always on time or early?   *YES/NO*

Do you find yourself clenching your teeth or fists, or drumming your fingers?   *YES/NO*

On holiday, is it really hard for you to just relax and abandon yourself to enjoyment?   *YES/NO*

If you answered 'yes' to three or more of these questions, you are probably suffering some stress symptoms already. If you answered 'yes' to five or more, you are probably a type A and should mimic type B characteristics, which are outlined on the opposite page.

'TYPE B' CHARACTERISTICS AND BEHAVIOUR

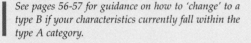

- Walk, move, eat and talk slowly
- Unfazed by delay
- Slow to anger
- Patient
- Happy to laze around
- Easy-going and non-pushy
- Unworried and unhurried by deadlines
- Work methodically at doing one thing at a time
- Composed and serene most of the time
- Content not to win at sport or card games
- Totally unconcerned about other people's opinions
- Relaxed about being late for meetings or dates
- Unambitious in the material or job sense

See pages 56-57 for guidance on how to 'change' to a type B if your characteristics currently fall within the type A category.

Hardiness – stress-handling characteristics

Over the years, certain characteristics in those people who handle stress well have been studied, and some fascinating information has emerged. A collection of personality traits have been identified called 'the hardiness factor', which are found in one combination or another in most individuals who are good at handling stress. Few people, however, possess all of these desirable characteristics.

Such people are usually thought of as being 'friendly', easy-going, avoiding confrontation and enjoying the company of others. In hundreds of studies, they have been shown to have a lower incidence of ill health of all sorts,

fewer heart attacks, less cancer and a much greater resistance to infection generally. They have variously been described as showing all or some of the following features – being open to new experiences, flexible, adaptable, extrovert, resourceful, full of enthusiasm, energetic, agreeable and kind-hearted, conscientious, diligent and dependable.

Are you just such an individual? One way of identifying such people is to see how many 'yes' answers you offer to the following questions – three or more probably means that the hardiness factor is well established in you.

Do you feel that you are able to influence positively the major events in your life?   YES/NO
(a 'yes' indicates a sense of control)

Do you tend to involve yourself wholeheartedly in whatever you are doing?   YES/NO
(a 'yes' indicates a sense of commitment)

Do you feel that life 'makes sense' in general, especially with regard to your own life?   YES/NO
(a 'yes' indicates a sense of coherence)

As changes occur in life (marriage, new job, new location, etc.), do you see such points of transition as a challenge rather than a threat?   YES/NO
(a 'yes' shows a sense of challenge)

Do you feel a part of your community and society in general, amongst like-minded people with whom you share a vision?   YES/NO
(a 'yes' equals community)

If most of your answers to these five questions are 'no', turn to pages 56-57 for ideas on how you might adapt your responses by actively adopting some hardiness characteristics.

ANALYSING OTHER STRESS FACTORS

Let's look at your life and lifestyle in order to better understand which areas might need modification over the months and years to come, so that you can set about acquiring a better state of health and sense of control over what affects you.

Some of these questions echo information given when we assessed specific health problems in the earlier pages of the book, and this might help you to link current health problems that you may be suffering from to your lifestyle and the choices you make each day.

By combining the information you get from the following questions with the ideas you now have about type A and B characteristics, 'hardiness' and the general effects of stress on your life, you should reach the point where you are ready to tackle the specific stress-inducing issues in your life with determination.

Most answers to the following questions, in an ideal world, would be 'no', so that 'yes' answers offer you clear signposts to action or clues to tendencies you may have. Keep a record and score of the *'yes'* answers under each heading.

Work stress
Do you work in a noisy, uncomfortable, poorly lit, crowded or dangerous environment?
YES/NO

Does your work involve physical strain, lifting, bending, etc.? *YES/NO*

Is your work stretching you to your limits?
YES/NO

Is your work unchallenging? *YES/NO*

Are there unpleasant interpersonal stresses at your workplace? *YES/NO*

Personal stress
Do you feel that there is not enough time in the day for your personal needs? *YES/NO*

Do you often feel that you are not appreciated and valued as a person? *YES/NO*

Do you feel that your life is boring? *YES/NO*

Are there severe interpersonal strains in your domestic/social life? *YES/NO*

Are there days when you touch no one and no one touches you? *YES/NO*

Time issues
Do you work more than eight hours most days of the week? *YES/NO*

Do you neglect to give yourself recreational time most days? *YES/NO*

Do you often neglect to give yourself a 'proper' lunchtime break? *YES/NO*

Do you do shift work? *YES/NO*

Do you regularly work to deadlines that are vital for you to meet? *YES/NO*

Self-care

Are there weeks in the year when you take no active exercise whatsoever?   YES/NO

Are there often weeks when you do no stretching (yoga type) exercise?   YES/NO

Are there many days when you don't go for a walk just for the sake of it?   YES/NO

Dependency issues

Are other people's opinions more meaningful than your own views?   YES/NO

Do you spend time pleasing others?   YES/NO

Are your plans for the future linked to someone else's future plans?   YES/NO

Have you lost social contacts because of a current relationship?   YES/NO

Do you modify your behaviour because of fear of someone's anger?   YES/NO

Addictive issues

Is it hard for you to express how you really feel about deep feelings?   YES/NO

Do you desperately crave a substance or food at least once every week?   YES/NO

Do you feel personally isolated and afraid of people in positions of authority?   YES/NO

Have members of your family had any substance addiction?   YES/NO

Do you enjoy crisis situations?   YES/NO

Habits

Do you use stimulants (coffee, tea, cigarettes alcohol) to 'get going' or to 'unwind'?   YES/NO

Would you answer defensively/aggressively if asked about your alcohol consumption, or another habit?   YES/NO

Would you find it hard to stop any of your social habits (alcohol, drug use, cigarettes)?   YES/NO

Has your work or have your relationships ever been affected by social habits involving alcohol or drugs?   YES/NO

Do you wake in the morning with a hangover at least once a week?   YES/NO

General and toxic stress

Do you drive in heavy traffic or have to use public transport most days?   YES/NO

Does your home or workplace have central heating, double glazing, air conditioning, and/or are the walls insulated with foam?   YES/NO

Do any of your hobbies involve use of chemicals, paints, glue, varnish, wood or brick dust or fumes of any sort?   YES/NO

Do you regularly have contact with pesticides, fungicides, chemical fertilizers, detergents, household or industrial cleansing and/or polishing materials?   YES/NO

Do you fly transatlantic or transcontinental more than once a year?   YES/NO

Do you drink tap water or cola/sodas/fruit juice with added sugar?   YES/NO

LIFE STRESS INFLUENCES ON THE BODY/MIND COMPLEX

As we examine the illustration on the opposite page, you can see at its centre an individual who represents any one of us, surrounded by many different sorts of stress – a complicated mixture of mind and body defences and repair activities, which together we call homeostasis. This word represents the way the body maintains balance. It is the way we cope with constant change, with challenge and with stress – by means of delicate balancing mechanisms which try to ensure that we stay healthy.

What is homeostasis?
● It is homeostasis which sorts out your circulation when you move from a hot room to the cold outside.

● It is homeostasis which decides what actions are called from your immune system when you catch an infection, to make sure you defend yourself adequately.

● It is your homeostatic mechanisms which ensure that your blood pressure equalizes when you get up from lying down.

In other words, homeostasis is actually the combination of the many functions and systems which defend, balance and generally sort out the specific needs of our individual bodies – without us even being aware of it.

Homeostasis is the combination of processes which have to deal with all the demands of the thousands of stresses that can affect us daily. When these defence and repair mechanisms are overloaded, when demands exceed the ability to adapt and cope, health problems occur.

Homeostatis overload
As adaptation fails, so illness starts. When this happens, when your health begins to deteriorate, it is not hard to realize that the best strategies will be those which:
● do not make matters worse
● reduce the stress load
● improve the way we cope by enhancing homeostasis

Stress load and the individual
As you look at the picture on the opposite page, you will not fail to realize that every one of us is being subjected to at least some of the stresses that this individual is having to deal with.

Because of the body and mind we have inherited, together with all that has happened to us in our lives to date, some of us will handle the 'stress load' as itemized more effectively than others. However, in the final analysis, every one of us would succumb to the stress load if it were heavy or prolonged enough. How we react to emotional situations; how well we are nourished; how much rest and exercise we get; how efficient our defence, repair and immune systems are – these are the vital factors in our defence against stress. A combination of reducing the stress load – ruling out specific stresses in our lives altogether or reducing them – and improving our defensive skills against them is the fundamental key to better health for everyone. The formula is obvious, once we have understood the nature of stress and its effects, and this understanding is a great help in our campaign to conquer stress.

In the following chapter of the book, we will look at specific ways of bringing about a reduction in our individual stress loads, together with effective techniques for improving our stress-coping strategies, to suit our own individual needs and lifestyles.

THE MULTIPLE STRESSES OF LIFE

Specific health problems – (13)
bowel, bladder ailments;
allergies; arthritis; pain;
fatigue, etc.

Acquired toxicity – (12)
atmospheric pollution,
drugs, etc.

Hormonal disturbances – (11)
menstrual, menopausal,
thyroid, etc.

Unbalanced lifestyle – (10)
poor eating habits; use of
stimulants such as coffee,
alcohol, cigarettes; poor
sleep patterns, etc.

In-born, genetic tendencies (9)
and problems.

Radiation hazards. (8)

Workplace stress – (7)
'sick- building' syndrome.

**Immune
and
defence
systems**

(1) Anxiety; emotional distress;
worries; poor self-esteem;
depression; work or domestic
or relationship problems, etc.

(2) Poor posture; muscle and
joint problems; physical
strain in work or hobbies.

(3) Chronic infections – viral
(herpes); fungal (candida);
bacterial (sinus, tonsils,
tooth problems); parasitic
(intestinal).

(4) Nutritional deficiencies
(vitamins, minerals,
essential fatty acids,
trace elements).

(5) Poor breathing habits; lack of
physical exercise.

(6) Addictive
behaviour/addictions.

CHAPTER FOUR

COPING WITH STRESS

You should by now have a clear picture of exactly what stress can do, how it is currently affecting you and some of the reasons why. In this chapter, we will explore some of the many very effective strategies you can adopt so that you are able to handle your stress in a more appropriate and safe way. This is where you can learn what it is possible for you to do, in order that you can begin to 'stress-proof' yourself.

LIGHTENING THE LOAD

There are many forms of stress, including those forces that influence us from outside and over which we apparently have no control, such as climatic change, pollution in all its forms, other people's behaviour, traffic, and so on.

Combatting 'outside' stressors
What we can do about the many different forms of stress that surround us is to:

● avoid what is avoidable – don't expose yourself to anything you can dodge, and protect yourself if you can't, e.g. avoid travelling outside or in peak periods; use an umbrella or wear warm clothing in the rain/cold, etc.

● alter your attitude to people's behaviour – regard people's sometimes aggravating behaviour as their problem not yours. Learn to respond appropriately, perhaps by taking assertiveness training, which teaches you to say what needs saying without anger.

● defend against pollution's effects – wear protective clothing/a mask and/or take antioxidant supplements, such as vitamin C, if exposed to pollution, for example.

Stress from within
Where stress is self-generated, produced by our own personalities and characteristics, we have a somewhat harder task in lightening the load. We need firstly to recognize, and acknowledge, that these features are indeed part of our makeup, and then we have to make the connection between the trait (being type A, for example) and stress. And finally, we have to want to change things – to begin the slow process of change.

Where you can identify factors in your life which are potentially stressful, perhaps by answering the questions on pages 36-37, or the type A & B questionnaires on pages 34-35, the way forward becomes clearer, but not necessarily easier.

Many of the behaviour patterns that are listed in these questionnaires are nothing more than habits we have learned, although we may have learned them in childhood. These can certainly be changed – slowly – by mimicking opposite forms of behaviour, and by slowly changing stress-inducing to stress-reducing actions.

Some behaviours are easier to change than others of course. For example, to a very large degree you can choose what you consume, i.e. whether you eat three balanced meals daily; drink too much coffee, tea, alcohol; smoke;

choose to drink tap water and the heavy metals, pesticide residues and petrocarbons it contains; use stimulants to boost flagging energy; or choose to use food supplements to assist immune function in its struggle with stress overload. You can also choose how much exercise you take, as well as what type; whether you overwork or insist on not taking work home with you, and many more such choices.

It is somewhat more difficult to suddenly decide to become a type B person – with all the 'hardiness' characteristics that are so desirable. As suggested, the way that these modifications can be incorporated into your behaviour is via a slow adoption of the characteristics you wish (and need) to acquire and, by practice and patience, gradually modifying towards the ideal.

Supplementary strategies

Stage by stage, step by step over a number of months, you can turn yourself from a frazzled, exhausted and highly stressed individual into a healthier, more energetic example of what you want to be.

During the stages outlined above, you should consider introducing choices made from the many methods of relaxation, which are detailed later on in this chapter. Try them all and settle for what suits you best.

You should, at the very least, undertake the following regularly (daily):

- one stress-reducing breathing method (pages 42-45), as well as
- one relaxation approach (pages 46-47), and eventually also
- one meditation and/or visualization technique (pages 50-55).

The key to success lies in doing what is possible, by appropriately reforming lifestyle, including your diet, rest and exercise routines as

MODIFYING BEHAVIOUR

PATHWAY TO POSITIVE CHANGES

- Evaluate your health status and summarize on paper those stress factors in your life that have been highlighted in the book so far. For example: 'family history of digestive and heart problems, and a current degree of chronic indigestion and excessive fatigue'.

- List the behaviour which may contribute to this. For example: 'eating too fast, skipping meals, not enough exercise, some type A characteristics'.

- Choose short-term goals and long-term objectives. For example: 'to improve digestion and reverse the type A behaviour'.

- Decide where you will start in this objective. For example: deliberately changing your eating arrangements and choices, and picking a type A behaviour (doing more than one thing at a time) as a starting place for change.

- Work at these changes for some weeks and reassess by evaluating a/ how you feel b/ whether change has taken place by copying type B approaches. If progress is noted, congratulate yourself and continue with the changes while considering the next stage of your transition towards a healthier stress-coping person, i.e. what are the next changes you will make?

needed in small stages; by avoiding artificial aids and stimulants (drugs, alcohol, cigarettes, etc.); by considering and using – according to your own particular needs – appropriate stress-reduction methods, as well as by allowing yourself pampering strategies (spoil yourself a little by having regular massage, aromatherapy, etc. – see pages 66-69).

CORRECT BREATHING

Before you can relax, your muscles need to be relaxed, and before this can happen effectively, it is helpful to learn to breathe in a particular way that makes the process of relaxation more effective. This also assists subsequent meditation and visualization, making these exercises much easier to perform. There are many breathing techniques, the first of which presented here is a marvellously efficacious 'anti-arousal' breathing method.

Research evidence
In research studies conducted in Holland, the USA and the UK, it was found that one particular sequence of breathing had the most powerful 'anti-arousal' effect compared with all others, and interestingly it was when an ancient yoga sequence – known as pranayama breathing – was used.

People were taught, and asked to practice, one of three different exercises:

1 Breathing in and out at the same rate.
2 Breathing in quickly and out slowly.
3 Breathing in slowly and out slowly.

After practising one of these methods, several times a day for some days, the people in the different groups were exposed to a variety of forms of stress, for example extreme noise, sudden temperature changes or mild electric shocks, and their responses were then studied. The researchers found that there was strong evidence of a benefit when only one of these breathing exercises was practised – the one in which there was a fairly rapid but full inhalation followed by a slow and controlled exhalation.

It was found that this method 'worked' only when practised regularly. It proved to be protective against stress – so much so that any stress to which the person was exposed a few hours after the breathing practice was handled better, although it was found that there was not much value in actually practising the method during the stress exposure.

This is just one of the breathing exercises which will be outlined in detail as a vital step towards more effective stress-handling, and part of the development of your protective shield against stress.

Anti-arousal breathing exercise
This is an exercise based on traditional yogic breathing, and the pattern is as follows :

1 Having placed yourself in a comfortable (ideally seated or reclining) position, exhale **fully** through your partially open mouth, with your lips just barely separated. This outbreath should be slowly performed.

   Imagine that a candle flame is just about 15 cm (6 inches) from your mouth, and exhale in such a way as to not blow this out but to just make the flame flicker.

   As you exhale, count silently to yourself to establish the length of the outbreath. An effective method for counting one second at a time is to say (silently) 'one hundred, two hundred, three hundred', etc. Each count lasts about one second.

2 When you have exhaled fully, without causing any sense of strain to yourself in any way, allow the inhalation which follows to be free and uncontrolled, and as full as it wants to be. The complete exhalation which preceded the inhalation will have created a vacuum to be filled, like a 'coiled spring', which you do not have to control in order to inhale.

   Once again, count to yourself to establish how long your in-breath lasts. The counting is necessary because the timing of the inhalation and exhalation phase of breathing is a very important feature of this exercise.

3 Without pausing to hold the breath, exhale **fully** again, through the mouth as directed in Step 1. Count to yourself at the same speed to time this phase of the breathing cycle.

4 Continue to repeat the inhalation and the exhalation sequences, as described above, for between a total of 15 and 20 cycles.

5 The objective is that in time (a few weeks in most cases), you should achieve an inhalation phase which lasts for 2 to 3 seconds, while the exhalation phase lasts from 6 to 8 seconds – without putting any strain on your body at all.

6 Remember that the exhalation should be slow and continuous. It is no use breathing out in two seconds and then waiting until the count reaches 6, 7 or 8 before inhaling again.

7 By the time you have completed 15 or so cycles, any sense of anxiety which you previously felt should be much reduced, and awareness of pain should also have lessened.

8 Repeat this exercise for a few minutes every hour if you are anxious, or whenever stress seem to be increasing. At the very least, it should be practised on waking and before bedtime, and if at all possible before meals.

Each time you finish your period of exercise, continue lying quietly for a minute or two.

ANTI-AROUSAL BREATHING

The anti-arousal breathing exercise can be performed with the hands resting on the abdomen. This can (a) help exhalation by gently pressing down on the stomach as you breathe out, and (b) sense the diaphragm working as the stomach pushes gently forwards on inhalation.

BREATHING EXERCISES

Apart from the very important pranayama anti-arousal breathing exercise described on the pages 42-43, there are other exercises that can be helpful and stress-reducing.

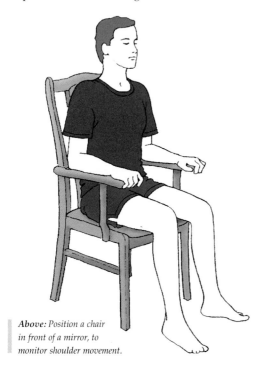

Above: Position a chair in front of a mirror, to monitor shoulder movement.

Preventing upper chest breathing

1 Find a chair with arms and position it in front of a mirror. Sit in the chair.

2 Breathe in deeply and observe your shoulders. Do they rise on inhalation?

3 If they do, you are inappropriately using an upper chest pattern when breathing and stressing the muscles of the neck, shoulders and throat (see page 28).

4 To start to correct your breathing pattern, push downwards with your elbows and forearms onto the arms of the chair as you inhale deeply. This will 'lock' your shoulders and force you to use your diaphragm as you breathe in.

5 Try to use the same timing described for the pranayama exercise (pages 42-43), that is a slow exhalation, and a free and unforced inhalation while your arms are pushing downwards against the arms of the chair.

6 Repeat 10 times, several times during the day.

Increasing lung capacity

1 Sit in an ordinary dining chair and allow yourself to slump forwards so that your left arm hangs between your legs and your right arm hangs outside your right leg.

2 Turn your head to the right as you inhale 'into' your upper right back, feeling the muscles in the area tighten as the lungs fill.

3 Hold your breath for between 5 and 10 seconds

4 As you slowly release the breath, stretch both hands towards the floor, which will stretch the upper back even more, then relax into your previous 'slump'.

5 Repeat this 5 times, and then alter your position so that your right arm hangs between your legs and your left arm hangs outside your left leg, head turned a little to the left.

Above: Try different angles of bend in order to stretch every part of your back.

6 Repeat the breathing and stretching 5 times, as previously described.

7 By altering the degree and angle of your bend, you can stretch different parts of the back of the rib cage, opening the rib spaces and increasing your lung capacity.

8 Do the exercise in at least two different slump positions for each side.

9 Sit for a minute afterwards until any sense of dizziness has gone.

10 Practise this breathing exercise daily.

Relaxation breathing

1 Lie supine on the floor with a pillow under your head and a rolled towel under the upper back and shoulders.

2 Keep your head straight with your arms at your sides, legs stretched out naturally.

3 Close your lips together, but keep them relaxed.

4 Breathe through your nose only.

5 Your breathing should be natural, but soundless, steady and unrestrained.

6 As you breathe in, think of the word 'quiet'.

7 As you breath out, think of the word 'relaxed'.

8 Consciously relax each part of your body in turn, from your head to your toes.

Try to remember that when you are practising breathing, it is important to focus your attention on exhalation – breathing out – and to let your inhalation be as free and uncontrolled as possible. If you empty the lungs, they will fill on their own, so practise the slow exhalation through your mouth, as described in the exercises, and then allow your lungs to expand and inhale freely, through the nose if possible, without trying to help this process.

Also remember that after performing any breathing exercise you might feel a little light-headed, so take care not to get up too quickly.

After completing the stretching/breathing exercise sitting in the chair for the first few times, you may feel some muscular soreness for a few days. Don't worry about this unduly; it is just the response of tight muscles being loosened, and will soon stop.

RELAXATION TECHNIQUES

It is not possible for a muscle to be both relaxed and tense at the same time, and so learning to release tension in muscles is a major step towards stress-coping.

When we respond to stress, our muscles tense (see pages 12-13) and over time this can become chronic, so that after a while we aren't even aware of the tension and certainly cannot just 'let go' and release it.

As a first step towards liberating ourselves from this state, we can use well-tried muscular loosening exercise methods, the best known of which is called 'progressive muscular relaxation' (see below). If you are very tense and you are asked to 'relax', you will probably tighten your muscles even more – mainly because you have forgotten what 'relaxation' feels like. It is as though you have forgotten what to do to achieve the release of tension in your own muscles.

Relearning relaxation
Relaxation has to be relearned. One efffective way to achieve this is to introduce a series of simple contractions or tightening efforts, which exaggerate the degree of tension in particular areas, so that as they are released you gradually become aware of the difference between 'tension' or 'bind' and 'release' or 'ease' of the area or particular muscle group.

Progressive muscular relaxation
Preparation: Wearing loose clothing, lie on a carpet or rug. Make sure there are no draughts, and that you are unlikely to be disturbed for about 20 to 25 minutes.

1 Lie comfortably so that your arms and legs are comfortably outstretched.

2 Tense the fist of your dominant hand and hold it in a tight clench for about 10 seconds.

3 Release your clenched fist and stay in this released state for about half a minute, savouring the sense of freedom, heaviness and release that you will experience.

4 Repeat this same muscle tension of your dominant hand at least once more before relaxing your grip and resting your hand in total 'ease' for approximately half a minute.

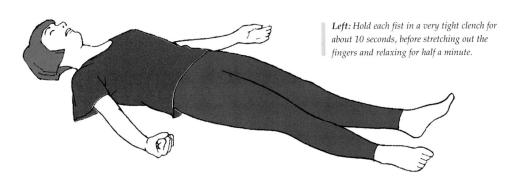

Left: Hold each fist in a very tight clench for about 10 seconds, before stretching out the fingers and relaxing for half a minute.

5 Repeat with the other hand at least twice.

6 Concentrate on your foot on the side of your dominant hand, and draw your toes upwards towards the knee, tightening the muscles and holding them tensed for 10 seconds.

7 Release and relax for half a minute, then repeat at least once more before going on to the other foot.

8 Perform this same sequence in at least 5 other sites (mostly bilateral, which makes an additional 10 sites), such as:

- backs of the lower legs – point the toes instead of drawing them up
- upper legs – pull the kneecaps towards the hips
- buttocks – squeeze them together
- chest/shoulders – hold an inhaled breath and at the same time draw the shoulder blades together
- abdominal area – pull in or push out strongly
- arms and shoulders – draw the upper arms into the shoulders strongly
- neck area – draw it into the shoulders or push it against the floor
- face – tighten and contract the muscles around the eyes and mouth, or frown strongly

Learning to recognize tension

Additional muscles can be dealt with in the same way by working out just what tightens them. The process of holding extreme tightness for a short period of time followed by complete release will, in time, create an awareness of what tension actually feels like, because you will have regained a point of reference, i.e. something to compare it with. This will enable you to recognize muscular tension as it builds up in your body, and to begin to prevent it happening before it becomes locked in.

After a week or so of doing these exercises daily (twice daily would be better still), you can start to combine muscle groups so that the entire hand/arm on both sides can be tensed and then relaxed together, followed by the face and neck, then the chest, shoulders and back and finally the legs and feet.

After another week, the tension element of the exercise can be abandoned, and you can simply lie down and focus on the different regions and note whether they are tense or not. You can then instruct them to relax.

Good results can be achieved quite quickly, but only if the exercises are performed thoroughly and regularly!

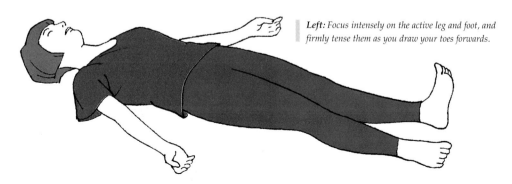

Left: Focus intensely on the active leg and foot, and firmly tense them as you draw your toes forwards.

SELF-STRETCHING TO EASE STRESS

Stress and tension make muscles tight, and tight muscles send a barrage of nerve impulses to the brain, reporting their over-stimulated status. When this happens, the brain/mind cannot relax, let go, calm down or become at ease.

Safe and effective methods
One of the ways of achieving more pliable, supple muscles is to regularly stretch them, in safe and gentle ways. Yoga offers such benefits, as does t'ai chi, along with enhanced breathing potential. If you can also perform some more active, aerobic type of exercise, you have the perfect combination for toning and relaxing the muscles of the body, as well as improving circulation through these tissues.

In order to get the most out of stretching, it helps to follow some basic rules which derive from yoga but which have sound physiological principles to back them up:

● Never force yourself beyond what you feel to be a comfortable stretch.

● Take yourself to the point of stretch in a given direction, and during an exhalation.

● While in this position of stretch, breathe slowly and fully 5 or 6 times (or up to a minute), and then, on an exhalation, make an attempt to achieve a slightly greater degree of stretch.

● Hold this new position for 5 or 6 breaths (up to a minute) before slowly coming out of the position.

● Never allow a stretch to be painful.

● Do your stretching exercises regularly!

First stretch position
1 Sit with both legs out straight in front of you and bend forwards, so that you can grasp one leg with each hand at a point where you feel stretch and strain in the low back as well as behind each leg.

2 Let your head hang forwards and down as far as is comfortably possible. There should be no pain – just mild discomfort as tight muscles are taken to their elastic barrier.

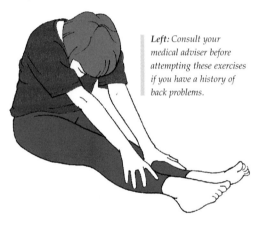

Left: Consult your medical adviser before attempting these exercises if you have a history of back problems.

3 Hold for a number of slowly performed breaths, and then, on an exhalation, stretch a little further and grasp the legs and hold for a further 5 or 6 breaths.

4 On sitting up again, bend one leg to place the foot alongside the other knee and ease yourself into a bend to grasp the straight leg. Exhale as you make the movement, and breath deeply as you hold the position for about half a minute.

5 Repeat the process of holding for a while and then bending further and holding again.

Above: Never stretch to the point of causing yourself pain.

6 After completion, change legs and stretch yourself down the straight leg, repeating the procedure as previously described.

7 After stretching down both legs individually, repeat the stretch in which both legs are straight.

This series of stretches effectively releases all the muscles down the back of the legs and the spine, as well as the neck.

Second stretch position

1 Sit on your heels and place your hands on the floor just behind your body.

2 As you exhale, bend backwards so that your pelvis and abdomen are pushed forwards. Allow your head to fall backwards to look up at the ceiling above you.

3 Hold this position for about 4 breaths, and then bend your arms to rest your weight on your fore-arms, arching your back slightly and with your pelvis pushed forwards.

4 Hold this for a further 4 breaths (about half a minute) as you sense the stretch along the front of your thighs, abdomen and front of the neck.

5 Slowly and gently come out of the stretch, and sit quietly for a minute or two and rest before resuming your normal activity.

Each of these stretches should be done at least once a day. Once you get used to doing these regularly, move on to other stretch sequences, of which there are dozens.

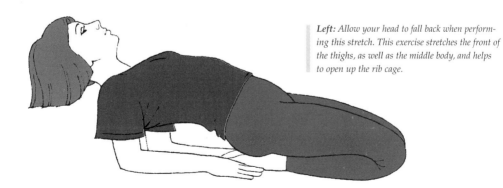

Left: Allow your head to fall back when performing this stretch. This exercise stretches the front of the thighs, as well as the middle body, and helps to open up the rib cage.

MEDITATION

For relaxation to work its magic on the body – to lower blood pressure, calm the nervous system, release tension in muscles, enhance immune system function and begin the process of reversing the damage caused by negative 'stress' emotions – both the body and the mind need to be in a state of stillness, calm and serenity.

The sequence

Before the mind can be calm, the body has to be relaxed, and before the muscles can release and relax, it is necessary for breathing to be regular, tranquil and easy. The ways to achieve these essential elements have already been discussed on the previous pages in this chapter.

Once breathing and muscle relaxation have been practised for some weeks, it is time to learn to meditate – to stop the mind being in a state of alert and alarm, to quit thoughts dashing about from topic to topic and to begin to let go and become tranquil. This procedure may sound esoteric and a bit offbeat, but meditation is actually a simple common-sense technique which anyone can learn and which many people do without knowing they are doing it.

Meditation occurs – and major health benefits result – when the mind is focused on just one thing, whether this is an idea ('God is love'), a word ('peace'), an image (a candle flame), a sound (a mantra which is a repetitive 'silent' sound repeated in your mind), a task (anything which requires focus – painting a wall or a picture, doing the washing up, gardening, etc.) or simply focusing on the thoughts which enter the mind without thinking about them. Meditation can only be effectively achieved when the muscles are relaxed and when breathing is regular and calm.

Preparing to meditate

Different forms of meditation suit different people. Some like active forms, while others achieve better results with a passive, reflective approach. The only way to find out what suits you best is to try various techniques, such as those listed on page 51, and judge whether you feel more relaxed, clearer in your own mind and more energetic.

Whichever you choose, first go through your usual breathing and relaxation routine, then adopt a posture which suits you.

Choose from the following positions:

- Lying on a carpeted floor, perhaps with a medium-sized book under your head to ease neck tension, spine flat (a small cushion under the knees helps if you have a hollow back).

- Sitting on the floor with your legs out straight and your back against a wall, gently resting your hands on your lap.

- Sitting cross-legged (tailor's position) with your hands resting on your knees, spine straight (a).

- Sitting on the floor in the lotus position (this is not easy unless you are flexible), (b).

(a)

(b)

- Sitting in an upright chair, hands on your lap (avoid slouching).

The wandering mind

Whichever position you choose, it should be comfortable, and make sure you avoid any feelings of strain. The key to meditation is keeping the mind focused on one subject/object. You should not become irritated when you find that your focus wanders onto other topics. Whenever you become aware that this has happened, you should simply refocus, gently, like a butterfly landing on a flower.

Another image which can be helpful is that of a pond's surface. You might visualize the surface of your mind as the surface of a pond, on which there are ripples (thoughts) which gradually get wider and wider as the surface becomes flat and calm, at which time your meditation object can once more receive your passive attention.

Different methods

Apply one of the following for at least five and ideally ten minutes daily at the end of your relaxation exercise.

- Sit or lie comfortably and let your eyes roll upwards towards your eyebrows. Hold this mildly uncomfortable state for about half a minute and then close your eyes, still looking upwards. Let the eyes relax and imagine that you can see an object – a candle flame, a cross, a circle of bright light – or anything else you can 'see' in your mind.

- Gaze at the centre of a candle flame some distance away from you, trying to maintain unblinking focus on it. After a few minutes, let the eyes close and keep focused on the after-image of the flame.

- Silently repeat in your mind a sound, such as 'om', until it takes on a rhythm of its own or becomes a drone – research has shown that using the word 'coca-cola' or 'banana' is as effective as using a traditional mantra.

- Repeat a meaningful (to you, personally) phrase, such as 'God is love', over and over again to blot out all other mental activity and to induce the condition of meditative calm.

- Focus attention on the tip of your nose, or back of your head, keeping either place as the object of your meditative attention.

- Observe the thoughts that are bubbling away in your mind. Observe these musings without thinking about them, and once observed, return to the surface of the quiet pond and await the next thought to enter your head.

- Hold something – worry beads, a few smooth pebbles or marbles – and feel their shape, texture and temperature with a slow rhythm as you move them from hand to hand or hold them in one hand. Focus attention on their particular characteristics; count them.

- Outside of your meditation exercises, try paying attention to the details of life, so that whatever task is at hand your mind is entirely focused on it. Be totally in the present – concentrate on what you are doing completely, on all sensations and feelings associated with your actions. This is what an absorbing hobby achieves, which is why they are so good for us.

Research findings

Research studies show that whichever form of meditation you choose to practise, when the mind is still and relatively inactive, alpha brain waves are produced and profoundly beneficial relaxation states can be achieved – resulting in anti-stress effects.

RELAXATION AND MEDITATION COMBINED

Relaxation exercises focus on the body and its responses to stress, trying to reverse these negative reactions (see pages 46-47), while meditation tries to bring about a calming of the mind – and through this a relaxation response. Autogenic Training (AT) combines the best of both approaches.

Autogenic Training exercise

The modified AT exercise described in detail below offers an excellent yet simple way of achieving effective relaxation.

Every day, ideally twice a day, for ten minutes at a time, do the following:

1 Lie on the floor or bed in a comfortable position, with a small cushion under the head, knees bent if that makes the back feel easier and eyes closed. Do one of the breathing exercises described on pages 42-45 for a few minutes before you start the AT exercise.

2 Focus attention on your dominant (say, right) hand/arm and silently say to yourself 'my right arm (or hand) feels heavy'.

Try to sense the arm relaxed and heavy, its weight sinking into the surface it rests on. Feel its weight. Over a period of about a minute, repeat the affirmation as to its heaviness several times and try to stay focused on its weight and heaviness.

You will almost certainly lose focus as your attention wanders from time to time. This is part of the training in the exercise – to stay focused – so don't feel angry. Just go back to the arm and its heaviness, which you may or may not be able to sense. If you can sense it, stay with it and enjoy the feeling of release – of letting go – that comes with it.

3 Next, focus on your left hand/arm where you do exactly the same thing for about a minute.

4 Move to the left leg and then the right leg for about a minute each, with the same messages and focused attention on each for about one minute.

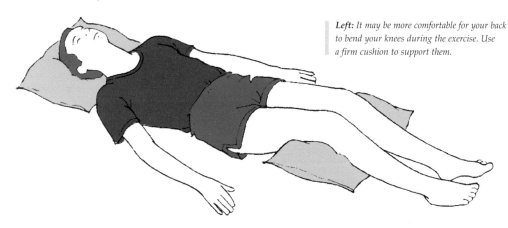

Left: It may be more comfortable for your back to bend your knees during the exercise. Use a firm cushion to support them.

5 Go back to your right hand/arm and this time affirm a message which tells you that you sense a greater degree of warmth there: 'My hand is feeling warm (or hot)'.

6 After a minute or so, go to the left hand/arm, then the left leg and finally the right leg, each time with the 'warming' message and focused attention. If warmth is sensed, stay with the sensation for a while and feel it spread over your body. Enjoy the feeling!

7 Finally, focus on your forehead and affirm that it feels cool and refreshed. Stay with this cool and calm thought for a minute before completing the exercise.

8 Finish by clenching your fists, bending your elbows and stretching out your arms. The exercise is now complete.

Successful results

By repeating the whole exercise at least once a day – it will only take approximately 10-15 minutes to complete – you will gradually find that you can stay sufficiently focused on each region and sensation.

'Heaviness' represents what you feel when muscles relax; 'warmth' is what you feel when your circulation to a certain area of the body is increased, while 'coolness' is the opposite – a reduction in circulation for a short while, in most cases followed by an increase due to the overall relaxation of the muscles.

Measurable changes occur in circulation and temperature in the regions being focused on during these Autogenic Training sessions. Success requires persistence – daily use for at least six weeks – before any significant benefits are noticed, usually in the nature of a profound sense of relaxation and better sleep.

Mind-calming

For a great many people, the use of Autogenic Training (AT) has been the best way of learning to calm the mind. Although ideas, sounds and images can be 'imagined' and focused on by many people, these can seem too 'abstract'. Trying to learn to focus on your hand or leg, especially if this involves a very common sensation such as 'warmth' or 'heaviness', is far more practical and meaningful somehow. In the end, whether you focus on an arm or an idea, the effect is the same – your mind will calm down and your body will follow it into a relaxed state.

Expert guidance

To learn AT properly, lessons may be needed from a fully trained expert. What has been presented on these pages is a simplified, safe version which anyone can learn to use, if they have the patience to spend just 15 minutes a day repeating the exercise. This is the 'training' part of Autogenic Training.

Common problem

The most commonly reported problem from people learning any form of relaxation or medition, including Autogenic Training, is that they cannot stay properly focused during the exercises. This is a normal occurrence, and it is important that you avoid getting angry with yourself when it happens. In fact, it is the very reason for the repetition of the 'training' involved in this method. When your mind begins to wander, and you become aware of this, bring yourself back gently to the focus called for – the heaviness of the arm, for example. In time, you will learn to stay focused, but it could take the regular application of the autogenic exercises over a period of some months before you achieve the ability to stay in one place for a minute without losing attention.

VISUALIZATION AND IMAGERY

Once you have learned how to rest at ease and to still the mind by using one or other of the various stress-reducing exercises presented on the previous pages, you can begin to travel adventurously using the imagery you can create in your own mind – in the same way as a brief but satisfying movie scene.

A few possible examples of visualization exercises and imagery are given on these two pages, which are specific to anxiety in particular and stress-reduction in general. Try performing them and see how effectively they might help you in your personal journey towards better stress-coping in your everyday life.

Basic steps for effective creative imagery

1 Set a goal: Decide on something that you would really like to realize or create – a life with less stress, perhaps.

2 Create a clear idea or picture: Create a clear mental image of the situation you would like to achieve in the present time already existing in the way you want it to be. Picture yourself in the situation and include as many details as possible.

3 Focus on the image often: Bring the mental picture to mind both in meditation and casually throughout the day. Try and focus on the image clearly in your mind, yet in a gentle way to avoid striving.

*Choose a comfortable position for your visualization exercises. This modified lotus position (**left**) is a good one. Alternatively, try sitting on your heels (**right**) with your hands resting on your thighs.*

4 Give it positive energy: Make strong, positive statements, suspend doubts or disbelief and give positive affirmations of achieving it.

Take a few minutes over each of the three example visualizations set out below and see how they might add another dimension to your relaxation exercises. Once you have the idea, you can begin to create your own images and pictures. Always try to complete one of your relaxation exercises (breathing, progressive muscular, meditation, etc.) with a visualization.

Anti-stress visualization exercise 1
Close your eyes. Breathe in and out a few times. Feel the restless need within your body to get up and move around or dance. Allow yourself to realize that as you have been looking at your restlessness, a vague image of flowers has hung in the background of your mind.

Attend now to those colourful images and notice that there are hundreds, growing in rings. There are vast rings and tiny rings, each flower nearly as tall as a human being and each swaying in place to a music only it can hear.

Before another thought can enter your mind, find that you are dancing with the flowers. Each and every one is danced with for a moment only, but there are many and it takes you a long time.

When at last you are finished, you realize that restlessness has been consumed by the ceaseless movement, and with its going, so has passed away your anxiety and tension. Take a moment to enjoy the peace, then allow your eyes to slowly open once again.

Anti-stress visualization exercise 2
Close your eyes. Breathe in and out a few times. Settle yourself into your deepest imagination, and remember a place that you have always enjoyed but haven't been to for some time.

See yourself in that place now and notice that you are not in harmony with its peace. See this disharmony as a faint shimmer of red and grey light where the image of you and the image of the peaceful place come together. Feel the disappointment that disharmony brings and ask your deeper self to help you relieve the situation.

Feel your attention drawn upward and see that a glimmering rain of violet light is descending upon you from out of the open air. Notice to your surprise that when the glimmer of violet touches the shimmer of red and grey, there is a brief release of energy, like the burst of steam when a drop of water hits a red hot pan. Just as the steam carries heat from the pan until it has cooled, the violet carries the shimmer from your body until you are in harmony and at peace.

Take a moment to enjoy your new-found peace and harmony, and then open your eyes.

Anti-stress visualization exercise 3
Close your eyes. Breathe in and out a few times. Imagine a bright, clean pool of water, deep in an untouched forest. Rain is drumming on the surface of the pool and realize that the shimmering of the water's face and the erratic reflection of the trees suits your mood right now.

As you gaze upon the surface, it seems natural to become one with the water, to identify with the pool. But as you become one with the pool, you realize that the pool itself is deeper than the disturbance upon its surface. This realization leads you to be aware of your own untouched depths, and you are surprised to discover that those depths – peaceful and harmonious – have been there all along.

As you have been within yourself, the rain has been slacking off, and now even the pools and your own surface have become less agitated. The rain stops altogether, and you are left serene and reflective. Enjoy, then let your eyes open.

'HARDINESS' AND 'TYPE B'

We know from the study of the link between the mind and the immune system that how healthy we are depends a great deal on our attitudes and reactions (see page 24). The more optimistic we are towards life in general, the better the chance we have of making a speedy recovery and a complete return to well-being.

Cultivating 'hardiness'

The characteristics of having a sense of control over your destiny, a feeling of commitment and wholehearted involvement when undertaking tasks, an attitude that 'life makes sense' and is coherent, that problems are challenges to be overcome not to be overwhelmed by, that you are part of a larger community of people and not isolated, and that you are involved rather than detached from society – these are all major elements in what makes someone 'hardy' (see pages 34-35).

One way of acquiring at least some aspects of these learned personality features is to mimic them, to 'pretend' that this is how you are and to see whether you can replace your present attitudes and responses with ones that fit better with these more desirable qualities. Over time, they can become habitual, and you may succeed in becoming more hardy.

For example, let's say you have bad news – something is happening or about to happen which has the potential to cause you harm or to change your life in some way which you don't want. Your normal reaction might be to brood over the situation, to think the worst, to bottle up your feelings and to feel yourself a victim. Instead of simply giving way to your customary responses, try to focus your mind on the following thought processes:

- Try speaking about how you feel to people who you know you can trust, even though normally this would be something you would definitely avoid doing.

- Try to look at the best possible outcome to the situation rather than dwelling on the worst consequences, and think about how you can actually, in practical terms, work towards achieving that end.

- Try to see what is happening in a wider context, not just how it relates to you and your life, and recognize that the situation needs to be dealt with suitably rather than simply being screamed about.

- Try to see what can be gained from the event, or threat – how you might be able to make the best of the inevitable consequences, to turn in a creative way a possible disaster in your life into a positive gain.

- Examine what actions you can take to modify the situation, to minimize the damage, alter the outcome and to exercise some control over events.

The consequence of actions such as these could bring about a lessening of stress for you and those around you, plus a greater sense of bonding with family members, friends and colleagues, as well as increased confidence when situations and events turn out not to be as bad as you had imagined.

There is evidence that we can change, over time, to a hardier, more resilient form of behaviour. It may not always be possible to do this alone, and you may require assistance – from a counsellor, or a psychotherapist, in one-on-one therapy sessions, or group/class exercise settings – but it can be done.

Mimicking type B behaviour

The same is true of anyone who is a type A (and all the health risks this carries – see pages 16-17 and 34-35), and who sees the need to change.

By observing the characteristics that make a type B, and by mimicking these one by one and taking time to acquire new behaviour patterns, type As have become type Bs and have secured, as a result, the health benefits that come with a more laid-back lifestyle.

The following are some of the changes you need to work towards:

- Listen to what people are saying and learn to respond appropriately (see pages 58-59 for details of assertiveness training).

- Don't allow anger to build. Learn to be able to express yourself without aggression.

- Do just one thing at a time.

- Copy how type Bs respond to situations that would usually make you explode.

- Appreciate that there is more to 'success' in life than just position and wealth, or that you need to struggle for this.

- Accept that you are human, that you are allowed to make mistakes and to be late or lazy at times – you do not have to be perfect.

- Forgive other people's shortcomings and poor behaviour – make allowances, and be more compassionate.

- Keep a watchful eye which triggers alarm bells inside when you start being bossy, aggressive and angry. Start to turn these responses around, to behave in a gentler way.

- Alter the way you work, reducing your load, avoiding deadlines, saying no to tasks that previously you would have added to your list of things to be done, etc.

One by one, in no particular order, the application of these changes in behaviour and attitudes will modify even the most dedicated type A into a far more pleasant, more healthy and far less stressed type B.

The hare and the tortoise

As you look at our type A hare and type B tortoise (see page 17) – not to mention our modified type A hare-cum-tortoise below – try to see beyond the comic side of the message, because in stress terms, there are few more important and potentially life-saving lessons to learn than the messages that these characters carry. This is all about the quality as well as the quantity of life. Tortoises live far longer than hares, and this is just as true for type Bs compared with type As.

With more time to watch the grass growing, and the opportunity to savour it to the full, your life will, in turn, become ever more pleasurable and full of meaning.

As type A hare characteristics slowly modify into tortoise-like behaviour, a host of nervous system, circulation, hormonal and other changes will slowly take place – leading to a healthier and happier existence.

ASSERTIVENESS

We learn behaviour and communication skills as we grow. The particular circumstances in which we develop, our home, school and social lives influence greatly how we learn to interact with other people. Whether we are aggressive, quick to answer and react; manipulative, submissive or always trying to please, our behaviour patterns with regard to our personal relationships, and in the context of our work, study, social and home settings, can be the source of many of the major stresses in our lives.

Assertiveness, in this context, has a precise meaning and significance. It is the term used to describe ways of communicating and behaving that are thought to offer the most effective and least stressful outcomes.

Stressful communication

Before looking at examples of the assertive approach, let's look at how some people are likely to handle different, everyday situations in ways that can produce unwanted stress for all concerned, and what the alternative assertive approach would be.

- **Submissive:**
  "I hope you don't mind but if it isn't too much bother, could you please try to send the book I ordered? Sorry to trouble you."
  Assertive alternative:
  "I ordered a book – could you please send it?"

- **Aggressive:**
  "You're being ridiculous. No one will believe a word you say, and who cares about your opinion anyway, so just shut up."
  Assertive alternative:
  "I disagree with your opinion."

- **Manipulative:**
  "If you are as fond of me as you say you are, I would expect you to try to please me by going to the theatre with me."
  Assertive alternative:
  "I want to go to the theatre – would like you to come with me?"

An assertive approach to a situation or person is direct, carries no hidden messages and is easy for the listener to interpret. It is quite straight-foward for anyone to learn to be assertive and therefore to communicate more effectively, with fewer mixed signals and misunderstandings, and therefore less stress.

Test your assertiveness

Make a note of your ticks for each of the following statements if you agree with them, and record a second tick for any statement if you believe that it applies to the way you now normally function and relate to others. The more double ticks, the more assertive you are currently. If there are only single ticks, these areas require work and you should consider undertaking assertiveness training.

✓ = try to be more assertive
✓✓ = good level of assertiveness

- It is OK to state your needs, irrespective of what other people expect of you.

- It is OK to state your opinion, irrespective of what is expected of you by other people.

- It is OK to say 'no' even when a 'yes' answer is expected of you.

- It is OK to make mistakes, and to admit these.

- It is OK to change your mind.

- It is OK to say that you do not understand something you've read or somebody has said.

- It doesn't matter whether people like you or not – you can still deal with anything that needs doing between you without experiencing either embarrassment or aggression.

- If you want something, you have the personal right to ask for it.

- You respect and honour anyone else who exercises these same rights.

- You expect to be heard and listened to, and conversely, you are prepared to listen attentively to what is being said to you.

By acquiring assertiveness characteristics in your dealings with others, you can become alert to submissive, manipulative and aggressive behaviour in yourself and others. You can also learn to avoid the many stresses that habitually emerge from misunderstandings between yourself and others.

Cultural differences

Stress can emerge from a failure to appreciate and respect how different cultures and societies shape the people that emerge from them. Each of us is the result of our own cultural, and social, exposure – whether this has been in an industrialized or rural setting, in a capitalistic, communist or some other society, whether in a matriarchal or patriarchal culture, in a well-off or deprived economic environment or from a religious or secular past. Legacies deriving from whatever background we come from can be major influences on how we handle those around us. If our relationships (work, home, personal, social, etc.) are less than happy, we should examine the gaps between what we believe, how we do things and the expectations of those with whom we clash or fail to work well with.

It might be that by understanding the background, the ethos and culture of others, we will have a better chance of stress-free relationships. Similarly, if others can understand our individual cultural idiosyncrasies, they might be better able to deal with us.

There are many sensitive areas, where religion, political beliefs, ethnic and culturally derived behaviours may clash. Assertiveness allows us to handle such variables plainly, without anger or aggression, without defensiveness and with the optimal chance of a stress-free resolution of problems.

Research has shown that the people who benefit most from assertiveness training are those who suppress their anger (except when dealing with children when they may shout and scream). Other signs that assertiveness training may be helpful include people who have a habit of making negative self-statements – always running themselves down. At the heart of such training is a need to 'immunize' against behaviour patterns which make feelings of inadequacy self-fulfilling, where a sense of 'not being as good as others' leads to people being dismissive or actually unkind.

To change this requires doing those things which demonstrate the positive as opposed to the negative aspects of life. An example would be to adopt an attitude which says: 'I might not be able to control life's events, but I can control how I think about and how I react to these events and situations, and therefore how I feel about what happens.'

This positive approach is precisely what the variety of behaviour modification techniques that are now established, such as assertiveness training, try to offer the individual.

LEARNING TO HANDLE TIME

How we handle time can produce stressful situations not only for ourselves but for others around us, either at home or in the workplace.

Your time demands

Consider how many of the following list of time-demanding possibilities (they occur or start at specific times) sound as if they apply to you. Record those that do with a tick.

Do you regularly (once a week or more):

• need to attend meetings?

• attend functions or assemblies (church)?

• have appointments to see someone (anyone at all, for either business or pleasure) where the start time for the meeting is fixed?

• have to prepare work to meet a deadline?

• have to prepare meals at specific times?

• have to be at work on time?

• have to prepare for examinations?

• have an obligation to visit sick relatives?

If you have recorded a tick for more than one of the questions above (and clearly the list could be easily extended), and especially if as you examined the particular time demand which you were ticking, you were aware of a sense of negativity – a sense that you wished strongly that you could be free of that particular burden – then that specific time demand is undoubtedly a significant stress in your life.

Your time-related stresses

Other ways in which time could be adding to your stress load will be indicated by the number of 'yes' answers you offer to the following questions – which in an ideal world would all be answered 'no'.

• Do you regularly (most days) find yourself doing more than one thing at a time?

• When performing a task (making a bed, writing a note, washing a cup, dialling a phone number), do you find yourself trying to get the task out of the way rather than trying to complete it slowly, thoroughly and efficiently?

• Do you get upset or impatient if there are delays – for example, when you are left listening to music or messages while waiting on a connection when telephoning; or when you are in a slow-moving line at the supermarket or post office?

• Do you get really upset by traffic delays?

• When you are doing something, do you really hate being interrupted?

• Do you find attending obligatory social events, such as weddings, meals with friends and family, etc., a 'waste of time'?

• When you are doing what you do best and the work is going well, do you insist on continuing whatever you are working on until you finish, ignoring all normal time constraints?

• Are you often told that you 'work too hard' (and do you secretly take a pride in this)?

• Have you virtually abandoned hobbies ('I love my work', 'Work is my hobby')?

• Do you regularly work more than five and a half days in a week?

- Do you regularly work more than 10 hours daily?

- Do you take less than two weeks holiday a year?

- Do you regularly take less than a total of half an hour for your midday meal?

The answers to all of these questions should be 'no', and in order to tilt your life towards a less stressful existence, modifications which turn stressful 'yes' answers into stress-free 'no' answers may be called for.

Rebalancing your life

You need to organize your life in such a way as to allow for more rest, relaxation, sleep and exercise, and above all to alter your attitude towards work and time. When you can see work obligations in their true context, as a part of a larger picture in which time usage is balanced to include regular breaks, and where hobbies and lazing around are part of your life, a less stressful situation in terms of your overall life will exist.

POSITIVE STEPS TO EQUILIBRIUM

- Apply rules which prevent you from overworking.

- Practise doing just one thing at a time, and doing it well, not starting the next task until you are well satisfied with the present one.

- An extension of the previous comment is to take particular interest in what you are doing, and to focus completely on whatever it is, making sure that the task is completed as well as you are capable of doing it – whether this is writing a report, cleaning a room, or stacking a shelf.

- Take regular weekend breaks away from home and your normal, everyday routines.

- Plan ahead for several months to include other activities such as bowling, dancing, camping, hiking, painting, theatre or whatever interests you, and make every attempt to fulfil these plans.

- Introduce some regularity into your sleep habits so that the healing and restoring qualities of sleep can help to reverse the wear and tear of life.

- When you are delayed (on the phone, in traffic, in line at the checkout), spend this time practising your slow breathing or contemplating a pleasant prospect – visualizing something really relaxing and pleasant.

- Start paying closer attention to what people around you say, carefully and thoughtfully.

- Cultivate a 'slow down' habit of movement and work, and discover that it is intensely satisfying – and often more efficient – to not have to rush.

RESTRUCTURING YOUR LIFESTYLE – EXERCISE

Some of the issues that arose from information gathered from questions asked on pages 36-37 have been partially discussed on pages 56-61, where hardiness and personality aspects, assertiveness training and time management were outlined. Other aspects of lifestyle stress – those linked to exercise, diet and toxic exposure – also need to be considered, so that you can have all the information available that will allow you to take actions to avoid the worst effects of this kind of stress.

Exercise issues
Exercise causes the release of hormonal substances which have a direct stress-countering effect, and it is therefore highly useful in helping us to handle stress more effectively. Some people, however, hate the very idea of exercise – and if you really dislike something badly enough, its enforcement as part of your life is likely to create more stress than it eliminates.

Perhaps a solution lies in looking at enough of the variations on the theme of exercise until you find something that really appeals to you.

Aerobics
There are two key areas which need to be examined – active exercise and slow stretching. Active exercising can involve working out at a gym, or participation in organized sport, or just as usefully could involve learning a dance routine – ballroom, Latin, folk, square dance, ballet, jazzercise, etc. – or simply acquiring and using a skipping rope or cycling, swimming or walking. In other words, regular stress-busting exercise can be applied at home, in a social setting or even as a solitary endeavour.

People who regularly exercise are not only physically fitter but are more 'emotionally and psychologically fit' than people who avoid exercise, according to American researchers who investigated the effects of aerobic activity on thousands of individuals. In some studies, it was shown that precisely the same calming effects which are achieved by meditation could be acquired by regular swimming, jogging, walking and yoga.

The key is not the type of exercise but the degree of regularity. Three sessions a week of not less than 20 minutes each, with never more than a two-day break in between, is the regime that is needed.

Finding your safety pulse rates for aerobics
There is a formula devised by the developers of aerobic exercising which you can use to discover what your particular aerobic levels are in order to get fit, and most importantly what you must not exceed to stay safe when exercising.

Everyone, at whatever level of fitness, can do cardiovascular training or aerobic exercise, but to be safe and effective you must do these calculations, substituting your own pulse rate and your own age for the numbers used in the example given below.

1 Take your morning resting pulse for a few days and find the average. In the example given here, we will say that it is 72.
Add this number to your age. If you are now 36, we have 72 + 36 = 108.

2 Subtract the number calculated above from 220 (220 – 108 = 112).

3 Calculate 60% (divide by 10 and multiply by 6) and 80% (divide by 10 and multiply by 8) of this number (112).

4 60% of 112 = 67

5 80% of 112 = 90

6 Add back your morning pulse to these two numbers (72 was our example).

7 67 + 72 = 139. When exercising, in order to achieve an aerobic effect, your pulse must be higher than 139 beats per minute.

8 90 + 72 = 162. When exercising, in order to perform aerobics safely, your pulse must not exceed 162.

When exercising, check your pulse regularly, either by means of a special pulse monitor (available from any sports store) or by learning to take your pulse for ten seconds and multiplying by six.

NB Remember to subsitute your own age and resting pulse for these example numbers.

These key numbers (139 and 162 in our given example) will change as you get fitter and older, because the numbers will alter – your resting pulse may get slower, and you will certainly get older. So remember to recalculate your safety pulse rate every year.

When taking your pulse, use one or two finger pads but **not your thumb**, since this has its own pulsation and will give a false reading.

Stretching

The other key exercise area is stretching, where many possibilities exist for use in groups or on your own. Pilates, yoga, T'ai chi, chi kung, Feldenkrais or Alexander training and Aikido are all options. The need to both tone the muscles of the body and to stretch them is important if you are going to make the best contribution to an anti-stress approach.

Some basic, highly beneficial self-stretching ideas, which you can perform easily at home, are presented on pages 48-49.

TAKING YOUR PULSE

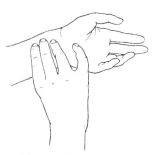

Above: *Look for your pulse just above the wrist crease below your thumb. Use a gentle pressure – no more than you can apply to your closed eye without hurting it.*

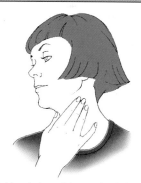

Above: *Feel just in front of the muscle which runs down your neck from behind your ear, just below the jawline.*

RESTRUCTURING YOUR LIFESTYLE – DIET AND NUTRITION

A comment from an unknown American physician contains a mountain of wisdom: 'All the vitamin C in the world won't make up for a bad attitude'. While this is certainly true, that more harm can be done to the body by emotional and personality burdens, it is also true that a well-nourished body can handle stress better than a badly nourished one.

Another way of seeing this is to understand that poor nutrition is itself a major form of stress. Studies conducted in the 1980s showed that the majority of people in industrialized countries (USA, Europe, Japan, etc.) were eating a diet which failed to provide them with all the essential nutrients required for good health in adequate amounts.

Soil contaminants

Most people tend to believe that a 'balanced diet' gives them all they need in the way of vitamins, minerals, etc. This is true in theory. However, the sad truth is that very few people actually consume a balanced diet nowadays, mainly because of the way food is produced. There is strong evidence that major changes have taken place in the quality of the soil in which our food is grown over the past 100 years, so that vegetables which were tested in the early 1900s can be shown to have contained up to 80% more zinc (as one example) than the same vegetables produced today.

Does this matter? Yes. To stay with the example of zinc, we know that many of our vital functions – including the efficiency of our digestion and our immune system – depends upon adequate zinc intake. And most important-ly, during periods of stress, we excrete more zinc than at times of peaceful calm. Similar examples can be given for most of the vital nutrients on which our health depends.

Over-consumption of sugar

Another major change in diet has been the vast increase in sugar intake, which has more than quadrupled over the past century. Sugar has a depressing effect on the immune system, and causes use of vast amounts of vital nutrients just to cope with its biochemical effects on the body. Sugar-rich foods can also have a major impact on mood. For example, swings can occur involving a 'high' after a sugar-rich snack or meal, followed by a dip into a low blood sugar state – at which time a quick fix of a sugar-rich snack (or a stimulant drink such as coffee or alcohol) may be used to push blood sugar levels up again. This switch back and forth of sugar levels is paralleled by mood changes ranging from exuberant to depressed, with cravings, extreme irritability and edginess in between.

Environmental toxins

A third major nutritional drain on the system occurs via the intake we have all been exposed to of toxic heavy metals such as lead, and aluminium, as well as of noxious substances derived from petrocarbons, which we breathe and absorb from the water supply. The body requires antioxidant nutrients (vitamins A, C, E, and the minerals selenium and zinc) to neutralize these dangerous substances – and modern Western diets are usually deficient in most of these vital elements.

The outcome of these imbalances is all too often a body which operates at a lower degree of efficiency – it digests and absorbs nutrients from food less effectively, detoxifies and eliminates wastes less well and repairs itself less successfully.

NUTRITIONAL DEFICIENCIES

● SIGN
corners of the mouth cracked
POSSIBLE DEFICIENCY   vitamin B

● SIGN
poor sense of smell and taste
POSSIBLE DEFICIENCY   zinc

● SIGN
excessive hair loss
POSSIBLE DEFICIENCY   protein

● SIGN
excessive bleeding of gums when cleaning teeth
POSSIBLE DEFICIENCY   vitamin C and/or zinc

● SIGN
tongue tip very red or tip very red
POSSIBLE DEFICIENCY   vitamin B complex

● SIGN
whites of eyes slightly blue
POSSIBLE DEFICIENCY   iron and/or vitamin C

● SIGN
fatigued and pale
POSSIBLE DEFICIENCY   iron and/or vitamin C

● SIGN
cramp at night
POSSIBLE DEFICIENCY   calcium and/or magnesium

● SIGN
rough dry skin at elbows and/or knees
POSSIBLE DEFICIENCY   vitamin A

● SIGN
no recall of dreams on waking
POSSIBLE DEFICIENCY   vitamin B6

Healthier eating options

If nowadays even a 'balanced' diet cannot offer optimum nutrition, and if sugar plays too great a part in many diets and if we are all overloaded with toxic debris, what can we do to restore some degree of balance? We can certainly make better choices as to what we eat and drink. For example, we can choose to adopt the following health-promoting measures:

● Purchase and eat organic vegetables and free-range ('wild') fish, poultry, eggs, dairy produce and meat, which reduces our chemical exposure. These are available from many supermarkets and specialist suppliers.

● Reduce our sugar intake as well as high-fat products, selecting instead products with no added sugar and those low in animal fats.

● Supplement – as an insurance against deficiency – a good-quality multimineral/multivitamin, which offers at least the recommended daily amounts of the essential nutrients which we need to survive and hopefully thrive in the increasingly toxic world in which we live.

● Eat an abundance of fresh fruits, vegetables, nuts, seeds, pulses and grains, which offer maximum nutritional advantages.

● Periodically (say, twice a month) place ourselves on a 'detox' day during which we eat only raw fruits and salads – to help improve digestive and detoxification functions.

● Ensure that we drink not less than 2 litres (3½ pints) daily of pure water.

● Avoid as much as we possibly can, those foods and drinks that contain added chemicals, preservatives, colouring, etc.

SELF-HELP STRESS REDUCTION – MASSAGE

Stress reduction can be achieved by lightening the stress load – strategies which remove or reduce those elements from your life which are making undue demands on you. Another way of helping to handle the load is to enhance your stress-coping abilities – by learning the essentials of relaxation, anti-arousal breathing methods, meditation, visualization, and so on.

A third approach is also available, which neither lightens the load nor uses the more obvious methods of stress-coping, but which simply increases the pleasure of living – which pampers, nurtures and coddles you. Such enjoyable methods include massage and/or self-massage and hydrotherapy using essential oils (aromatherapy).

Massage and self-massage
Research at the famous Touch Research Institute, a part of the Miami School of Medicine, has shown that regularly receiving and giving massage – even simple, unprofessional stroking – has profound stress-reducing effects. When grandparents were instructed in how to massage their grandchildren using very simple methods (see below), not only were stress markers in the children improved but the blood pressures of the grandparents were reduced and stress levels decreased.

Many people are not touched enough, and being touched in a caring and compassionate way is health-promoting and stress-reducing. Applying self-massage at least once a week is one option, or getting a friend or close family member involved is another. Additionally, treat yourself periodically to a professional massage, when circumstances allow.

The rules for applying massage and self-massage are simple and straightforward:

- Strokes should be applied using a light lubricant – a few drops of a soothing essential oil, such as lavender, cedarwood or chamomile, combined with a carrier oil, such as soya, sesame, sweet almond, wheatgerm, or something more luxurious such as coconut, avocado, jojoba, peach nut or apricot nut.

- The hands should start by slowly and rhythmically stroking the part of the body being treated – gliding, circling, lifting, wringing and stroking the back, legs, shoulders, arms or wherever tension is most obvious.

- Using the whole hand, muscles can be gently lifted and stretched – painlessly wrung and squeezed (in the same way as getting water out of a towel).

- Alternatively, a series of alternating whole-hand strokes can be applied, in which one hand slowly and rhythmically pushes the tissues away, while the other hand draws adjacent tissues forwards, so gently lifting and squeezing the tissues.

- Fingers and thumbs can be used to gently 'tease out' tight areas, while light 'feathering' strokes can be applied to end the 'treatment' of particular areas.

- No pain should be caused, and the massage should be slow and pleasant. Never perform a massage in a hurry or when you are feeling in any way agitated – you will not get a good result.

MASSAGE TECHNIQUES

MASSAGE

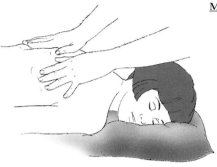

Above: If, when your hands are circling, kneading and rubbing the back in a rhythmical way, you come across areas of pain – which is very probable – don't be tempted to dig into these muscles unless you have trained in massage. Just try to relax the area.

Above: There are few more relaxing sensations than a good foot massage. Hold the foot firmly at the heel, for example, and work with the thumb and fingers in a slow, intentional way. Keep the pressure modest, since there is only a shallow layer of muscle on the foot.

SELF-MASSAGE

Above: Whole hand actions which grasp and stretch the muscle, as well as finger and thumb-tip pressures, are equally useful. Always finish a massage sequence with a soothing 'rubbing' sequence, which helps to drain the muscle tissues as well as calm the nerves.

Above: This is very different from having a relaxation massage applied to you, since you can use a safe degree of pressure and discomfort on yourself to 'work' tense, tight muscles – around the base of the neck especially – without any danger of doing harm.

SELF-HELP STRESS REDUCTION – AROMATHERAPY / HYDROTHERAPY

Adding essential oils to bathing water is another effective and highly pleasurable way of inducing deep relaxation.

Essential oils

Essential oils are derived from different parts of plants – flowers, leaves, bark, berries, stems and roots. Parts of the same plant may produce various oils. These oils have been shown to produce specific and general physiological effects – with some having profoundly relaxing influences on the mind and body.

These oils can be purchased from many retail outlets, especially specialist pharmacies, cosmetic stores and healthfood stores which have pioneered their marketing.

Using essential oils

When using oils in the bath, no carrier oil is mixed with the essential oil – it is placed neat into the water while it is running. About 10 to 15 drops is an ample amount – either of a single oil or a combination of two or more oils. Lie back and enjoy the experience for a minimum of 15 mintues. Vetiver, chamomile, lavender and neroli are all relaxing and useful for anxious, stressful situations. See the panel on the opposite page for further details on some specific stress-beating oils and how they can be used.

Another way of using these oils is to apply them directly to the skin after a bath or shower in which the pores have opened. It is usually suggested that, as with massage (see pages 66-67), a few drops of the selected oil be mixed with a carrier oil (almond, sesame, etc.), since neat oils can be too concentrated to be placed directly onto the skin.

An additional, extremely therapeutic way of using essential oils is as room vaporizers, when the scent is gently dispersed and you are barely aware of breathing it in. Commercial burners are available which consist of a small container that should be filled with water and up to five drops of essential oil added. This is then placed above a lighted candle or nightlight.

Essential oils are usually supplied in dark glass bottles, and should be stored in a cool place and out of direct sunlight.

Neutral baths

While many people seem to enjoy hot baths and find these 'relaxing', the fact is that heat is exhausting and stressful.

The most relaxing of all baths is the 'neutral bath', in which the water is more or less equal to body temperature. Such baths taken before bed-time have been shown to produce a deep relax-ation and better sleep.

For the best effect, a period of around 20 min-utes should be spent relaxing in a neutral bath, with as much of the body submerged as possi-ble. Periodic topping up with hot water is usual-ly necessary to prevent the water getting cold. It is also important to ensure that the bathroom is warm, so that getting out of the bath is not a shock to the body.

By combining a neutral and an aromatherapy bath, a doubly relaxing effect can be achieved.

Flotation relaxation

By combining the profoundly relaxing effects of a neutral bath with the semi-weightless state achieved by increasing the density of the water – simply by adding Epsom salts – it is possible to mimic the effects of a flotation tank.

In a flotation bath, you are suspended in buoy-ant, neutral temperature water inside a light-proof tank to remove external stimulus.

In your own home, you can run a neutral bath and into this dissolve ½-1 kilo (1-2 pounds) of commercial Epsom salts (most pharmacies will supply this). As you rest in the bath, wear an eye mask to cut out light and so reduce outside stimulus even more.

The benefits of this have included reduced anxiety, depression, fatigue, pain and feelings of tension and frustration.

After any Epsom salts bath, you should rest for several hours and may perspire heavily. Note that you cannot use such a bath to wash, since no soap will lather. You should shower after the use of Epsom salts if you want to avoid sweating. The best advice is to have such a bath, pat yourself dry and go to bed for at least a few hours, and to let the detoxification benefits of sweating take place.

ESSENTIAL OILS

Lavender:
Used in the bath, lavender oil can help to alleviate stress and combat insomnia.

Massaging with lavender oil promotes deep relaxation in the body.

For a soothing foot massage:
4 drops lavender oil and 3 drops rosemary oil in 20 ml (4 teaspons) carrier oil.

Neroli: Excellent for treating both long-term tension and short-term stress.

Neroli oil makes a wonderfully calming, scented bath.

For a tranquilizing bath: *2 drops neroli oil, 2 drops rose oil, 2 drops lavender oil and 2 drops ylang ylang oil.*

Ylang Ylang: With its strong, sweet floral aroma, ylang ylang oil is hypnotic and relaxing.

Good for helping to relieve emotional turmoil.

For a calming body massage: *4 drops ylang ylang oil, 3 drops jasmine oil and 2 drops geranium oil in 20 ml (4 teaspoons) carrier oil.*

Chamomile:
One of the gentlest and most soothing of all oils. Its sedative effects can benefit those suffering from headaches. Chamomile oil mixes well with cedarwood, eucalyptus, jasmine, geranium and frankincense.

In a warm bath, chamomile oil is a marvellous antidote to everyday stresses and strains.

For massaging aching feet:
2 drops chamomile oil and 2 drops eucalyptus in 20 ml (4 teaspons) carrier oil.

Peppermint:
With its strong, menthol smell, peppermint oil is stimulating and helps overcome fatigue.

Peppermint oil is ideal for a footbath or foot massage.

For a stimulating body rub:
1 drop peppermint oil, 1 drop myrrh oil and 2 drops lavender oil in 20 ml (4 teaspoons) carrier oil.

STRESS STAIRCASE

The 'stress staircase' shows how with sufficient stress a threshold is eventually crossed, at which time illness develops. In this representation of the build-up of possible stresses, we can see on the side opposite to some of the listed stresses various counter-measures or treatment options. For example:

- The key 'treatment' choice for nutritional deficiency (a major stress influence) would be sound nutrition and possibly the use of supplementation.

- The answer to postural stress would be to adopt bodywork of one sort or another, as well as taking up exercise, stretching, postural re-education, etc.

- Approaches which would counter emotional and psychological stress factors would include many of the relaxation methods already discussed in this book, as well as counselling, psychotherapy, etc.

Lessons to learn

Three important messages emerge from this schematic view of stress influences – the stress staircase:

- As a rule, harm derives from an accumulation of different stresses.

- The particular mix of stressors that affects you is unique to you.

- There exists a wide range of 'answers' and defences to most of life's stresses, many of which are available from complementary

healthcare providers, and in main-stream medicine (see pages 72-73 for details).

- Many of these answers actively involve you in the healing and recovery process, and so increase your sense of 'control' over your life – an essential part of developing 'hardiness' characteristics (see pages 56-57).

Cautions to consider when seeking complementary treatments

- When seeking advice from an 'alternative' or 'complementary' practitioner or therapist, always ensure that whoever is consulted is suitably qualified and/or licensed.

- If you already suffer from a medical condition which is receiving conventional attention, it would be wise to discuss your interest in seeking alternative/complementary attention with your usual medical adviser, and to discuss in full your medical condition and the treatment you are receiving with anyone else you consult.

The things which make us ill are found in the many stress factors listed on the left-hand side of the staircase. Some of these are beyond our control (we are born with them), while others are well within our control – in the choices we make in what we eat and do. When enough of these stress factors are working on us, symptoms start and health declines. We can either reduce the load or improve how well we cope with the load. Better still, we can do some of both, and the many forms of self-help and complementary healthcare can go a long way towards achieving both objectives. Study the stress staircase, and consider what you might do to reduce the load on yourself and to improve how well you can cope with what you cannot escape from.

STRESS STAIRCASE

Threshold at which adaption capacity is exhausted and disease becomes inevitable

Problems with other people – poor self-image, isolation, anxiety	Stress-coping skills – counselling, relaxation, bodywork
Poor coping skills Type A personality	
Lifestyle, habits, e.g. alcohol, smoking, lack of exercise	Reforming lifestyle Immune support Supplementation Acupuncture Herbal and homeopathic care Prayer; spiritual awareness
Immune system decline through illness	
Negative environmental influences – Radon gas, for example	
Lack of purpose; spiritual deficiency – no beliefs or hopes	
Structural stress – poor posture, injury, bad breathing habits	Bodywork Body reeducation Balanced diet Supplements Fasting Detoxifying
Deficiencies – vitamins, minerals, etc.	
Acquired toxicity through food, water, air, drugs (lead, pesticides, etc.)	
Poor early family factors – abuse, divorce, poverty	Homeopathy Clean environment Detoxifying
Childhood illness – no breast feeding	
Genetic factors – problems we are born with	Probiotics, Optimal nutrition, Sound hygiene Stress-free environment

Good health, sound immune system, intact homeostatic function, symptom free

Within this framework, which will be individual to everyone, are also to be found influences of viruses, bacteria, yeasts and parasites – some essential to life and many a threat to it.

Depending on the intensity and duration of these multiple stressors, symptoms will begin to appear, sooner or later. They are evidence of repair and defence mechanisms in action.

COMPLEMENTARY HEALTHCARE OPTIONS

By applying the guidelines given on previous pages, as well as selecting, if appropriate, from the complementary healthcare choices discussed on these two pages, you have the chance to slowly but surely turn your life around and aim for a healthier, less stressed existence.

Please note that the research evidence supports the therapeutic/stress-reducing value of all the methods listed below.

Aikido: One of the many martial arts which (as with most of these methods) encourages a sense of control, focused awareness and self-confidence.

Acupuncture/acupressure: Traditional Chinese methods which ease pain and muscular restrictions, and which attempt to 'rebalance' energy disturbances.

Alexander technique: A postural reeducation system which, over months of lessons, teaches you how to use your body more efficiently, with less strain. Alexander lessons are extremely relaxing. *See also Feldenkrais below.*
Associated methods, which have common elements with Alexander, include Postural Integration, Mensindieck system and Hanna Somatic Education.

Aromatherapy: Utilizes a combination of massage and essential oils with proven therapeutic effects. The stress-reducing and relaxation influences of aromatherapy have been established by research.

Autogenic training: Helps your mind to learn to influence your body processes (such as circulation or muscle tension) at will, and encourages deep relaxation. It combines elements of meditation, and guided imagery (visualization) – *listed below.*

Biofeedback: Uses information-gathering machines (blood pressure, for example) which provide your mind with a specific focus, enabling (as in *Autogenic Training*) you to learn to influence body processes. In doing so, profound relaxation occurs.

Bodywork: Chiropractic, osteopathy, massage, soft tissue manipulation, neuromuscular therapy, physiotherapy and others, which use manipulation and exercise methods to normalize and rehabilitate body mechanics. Massage in particular has been well researched to show its anxiety-reducing effects. Physiotherapy, osteopathy and chiropractic have been widely used to help normalize and retrain postural and breathing dysfunction.
Other methods which complement bodywork include Connective Tissue Massage, Muscle Energy Technique, Myofascial Release techniques, Positional Release techniques, Tragerwork, Hellerwork, Rolfing, Aston Patterning and Soma Neuromuscular Integration.

Chiropractic: *See Bodywork.*

Counselling: Encourages you to learn about yourself, to know why you do what you do and to gradually allow you to come to an awareness of more life-enhancing ways of thinking and behaving. Counselling does not attempt to provide answers to life's stress-inducing problems, but encourages you in ways of finding these.

Craniosacral therapy: Very gentle manipulation, focusing particularly on the head and low back, which has profound relaxation influences.

Exercise: All the options, from dance through skipping to jogging, cycling and gym classes to walking, help produce hormonal and muscular changes which are profoundly anti-stress if applied regularly (three times weekly for a minimum of 20 minutes) – *see also Pilates, Yoga and T'ai chi.*

Feldenkrais: Helps you to regain coordinated, efficient and easy communication between the brain and the body.

Guided imagery: *See Autogenic Training and Visualization.*

Herbal medicine: Uses plant-based remedies to help the self-healing mechanisms of the body (homeostasis) to work more efficiently.

Homoeopathy: Uses minute doses of medicines to stimulate the body's self-regulating mechanisms. Homeopathy claims to beneficially influence both inherited as well as acquired health imbalances.

Hydrotherapy: A variety of safe and well-tried water treatments exist which can influence body functions (circulation, detoxification, etc.), or which can be used to produce relaxation effects.

Meditation: Learning to focus the mind is the key single common feature of all the many different meditation systems (the best known of which is Transcendental Meditation – TM), which produce a relaxation response that counters stress responses. Daily practice is suggested for major benefits.

Naturopathy: Focuses on reforming lifestyle habits (diet, exercise, breathing retraining, sleep patterns); uses fasting (detoxification), nutritional, hydrotherapy, bodywork, herbal and other approaches to encourage self-regulating mechanisms of the body.

Osteopathy: *See Bodywork.*

Physiotherapy: *See Bodywork.*

Pilates: Widely used approach in the performance arts, its full name is 'Pilates Physical Mind' method. Combines rhythmic stretching and strengthening involving special equipment, usually under the guidance of a trained instructor. Regular application produces a calmer mind as well as a more supple and efficient body.

Polarity therapy: An extremely gentle and relaxing approach to rebalancing the electromagnetic energy which surrounds and permeates the body.

Psychotherapy: There are a number of forms of psychotherapy which aim mainly to increase self-awareness and build stress-coping abilities.

Reflexology: Manually treats reflex areas, usually on the hands and feet, in order to influence body systems and functions.

T'ai chi: Traditional Chinese rhythmic, slow, exercise system which encourages improved breathing, balance, coordination, posture and relaxation. Only effective if regularly applied.

Therapeutic touch: A modern name for 'healing'. Usually applied without touching the body, by someone who is themselves centred and relaxed. Research shows it to have strong anti-stress effects.

Yoga: Traditional Indian system which incorporates breathing and stretching. Produces profound relaxation effects if applied regularly.

Visualization: Once the mind is still *(see meditation and guided imagery)*, it is possible to guide it towards health-enhancing images and deeper relaxation. Autogenic training combines both meditation and visualization.

Others: A range of additional energy-balancing and body/mind integration methods exist, e.g. Chi Kung, Rosen Method, Somatosynthesis, SHEN, Hakomi, Jin Shin Do, Reiki and Zero Balancing.

USEFUL ADDRESSES

Association of Reflexologists
27 Old Gloucester Street,
London WC1N 3XX
Tel: 0990 673320

The British Chiropractic Association
29 Whitley Street,
Reading RG2 OE9
Tel: 01734 757557

British College of Naturopathy and Osteopathy
6 Netherhall Gardens,
London NW3 5RR
Tel: 0171 435 6464
Fax: 0171 431 3630

British Complementary Medicine Association
St Charles Hospital, Exmoor Street,
London W10 6DZ
Tel: 0181 964 1205

British Herbal Medicine Association
PO Box 304, Bournemouth,
Dorset BH7 6JX
Tel: 01202 433691

British Homeopathic Association
27a Devonshire Street,
London W1
Tel: 0171 935 2163

British Nutrition Foundation
52-54 High Holborn,
London WC1V 6RQ
Tel: 0171 404 6504
Fax: 0171 404 6747

Institute for Optimum Nutrition
Blades Court, Deodar Road,
London SW15 2NU
Tel: 0181 877 9993

**International Society
of Professional Aromatherapists**
ISPA House, 82 Ashby Road, Hinckley,
Leicstershire LE10 1SN
Tel: 01455 637987

The London College of Massage
5 Newman Passage,
London W1P 3PF
Tel: 0171 323 3574

**The London School of Acupuncture and
Traditional Chinese Medicine**
60 Bunhill Row,
London EC1Y 8JS
Tel: 0171 490 0513

**The London School of T'ai Chi Chuan and
Traditional Health Resources Ltd**
45 Blenheim Road,
London W4 1ET
Tel: 01426 914540

National Institute of Medical Herbalists
9 Palace Gate, Exeter
Tel: 01392 426022

Society of Homeopaths
2 Artizan Road,
Northampton NN1 4HU
Tel: 01604 21400

The T'ai Chi Union for Great Britain
69 Kilpatrick Gardens, Clarkston,
Glasgow G76 7RF

Yoga Therapy Centre
60 Great Ormond Street,
London WC1
Tel: 0171 833 7267

INDEX

INDEX